RAVE REVIEWS FOR
ANDREW COBURN!

"Natural storytellers are not too common, but Mr. Coburn is one."

—*The New York Times*

"There is a Hitchcockian flavor to Andrew Coburn's thrillers. He has a good eye and a great ear and his people ring true."

—*The Boston Globe*

"For cold-blooded menace, Coburn goes from strength to strength."

—*The London Observer*

Coburn's "dialogue is perfect, sometimes acidic, and always intelligent."

—*Chicago Tribune*

"Coburn's tough as Dashiell Hammett and plots and writes with the skill of Graham Greene."

—*Newsday*

Coburn's "characterizations are pitch-perfect, something out of Larry McMurtry."

—*St. Louis Post-Dispatch*

ONLY A MATTER OF TIME

Sherwood, considered state of the art, was a youth detention center situated well west of Boston. Bobby Sawhill entered it in July, which distressed Chief Morgan. "My fault," Morgan said, dropping wearily into a chair near Meg O'Brien's desk. "A double murder charge, he'd have been tried as an adult, no question about it. Now he'll walk when he turns twenty-one."

"Foolish to blame yourself," Meg said.

He knew no one else to blame. He'd been suspicious about Mrs. Bullard's death but had never followed up. A better policeman would have, he told himself.

"You don't know for sure," Meg said.

Morgan said, "Yes, I do. In my gut. What I don't know is why. Why Eve Bullard? Why Claudia?" His voice was thin, clinical, without skin.

"Don't drive yourself crazy," she said.

He smiled. "You know what I also know, like it's written on a blackboard?"

She knew and didn't want to be told. "You could be wrong."

"No, Meg. Sure as I'm sitting here, he'll kill again."

ANDREW COBURN

ON THE LOOSE

LEISURE BOOKS   NEW YORK CITY

For Ed Gorman:
A finely tuned writer
and a courageous fellow.

A LEISURE BOOK®

February 2006

Published by

Dorchester Publishing Co., Inc.
200 Madison Avenue
New York, NY 10016

ISBN 0-8439-5671-2

The name "Leisure Books" and the stylized "L" with design are trademarks of Dorchester Publishing Co., Inc.

Printed in the United States of America.

Visit us on the web at www.dorchesterpub.com.

ON THE LOOSE

CHAPTER ONE

Mrs. Bullard's white hair was wild. A free spirit all her life, she wore a bra top and skimpy shorts and stood on stiletto heels amid her late husband's rose bushes. She was probably the tallest woman the boy had ever seen. More than six feet in her prime, Mrs. Bullard had shrunk scarcely an inch in old age. Bones jutting sharply at uncommon angles made her body look feral. Despite her eighty years, she considered herself a woman to be reckoned with and a match for any man. The boy was an intruder in her garden.

"Bobby," he said when she asked his name. She didn't need to be told he was a Sawhill. Sawhills had been in the town when the flag had thirteen stars. His grandfather, whom she might have married had she not chosen a Bullard, had once told her she had the warmest backside of any woman he knew.

"How old are you, Bobby?"

"Twelve," he said, which would have been hard

to guess. He was big for his age and had a crew cut that squared his head and extended the fullness of his face, which remained a baby's.

"What are you doing here?" she asked, and he claimed the gate had been left open, a fib she let pass. "You're a long way from your neighborhood. Don't you have friends to play with?"

"I don't have any."

"That's hard to believe," she said kindly and falsely. She suspected he was vulnerable and knew he was motherless, his father an alcoholic for whom sobriety was a strain after a week and an impossibility after two. She said, "I knew your grandfather."

He gazed off at a finch feeding on thistle. His grandfather, dead before he was born, obviously did not interest him. Abruptly his voice sprang at her. "Did you know my mother?"

She conjured up an image of a woman with eyes bluer than most blues, the only visible link to the boy, who in other respects was a Sawhill, from the smooth swell of his brow to the tight set of his feet. "Not really, Bobby. Your mother wasn't from Bensington."

"She was young," he said aggressively.

"Yes. Your father, like your grandfather, married late but chose young."

"You're old."

"No getting around that," Mrs. Bullard said with a wistfulness that almost amused her. "Would you like to help me weed?"

Without warning, shocking her, he plucked a

rose and scattered the petals. Her husband had nursed the roses from season to season, feeding them in autumn, protecting them in winter.

"If you want to be welcome here, you won't do that again," she said, trembling. Her husband had died nearly seven years ago, but in her mind it could have been yesterday. In her dreams the dead mingled with the living and carried on in a world beyond death, proof enough of an articulation between this life and the next. "Did you hear me?"

He nodded absently while watching the finch fly away. He was a Sawhill, but he lacked his grandfather's manners and charm.

"When I talk to someone," she said sharply, "I expect to see the front of a face, not the side."

Suddenly facing her, he mocked her with his eyes, in the blue of which his childhood seemed compressed, squeezed of its essence. For an unsettling moment she felt they were on equal footing.

"You'd better go now," she said.

"Why?"

"Because I say so," she said, her patience gone. She had never had a child of her own, only a niece. A daughter would have pleased her, but she'd always had doubts about a son.

"Can I come back?" he asked.

She didn't want the bother. Besides, much about him looked untrue, unreasonable, as if like his father he were a Sawhill in weak ways. "There's no point."

He turned without argument, shuffled beyond the roses and paused near the pink radiance of phlox. Looking back, he said, "I just saw a snake."

"Good," she said. "Snakes eat bugs. Bugs bother flowers."

Alone, wearing garden gloves, she weeded for only a few minutes. Crouching disturbed her spine and cramped her long legs. The sun cooked her. She craved the cool of her house. The house was gingerbread, more or less Victorian, painted pale blue. In slight disrepair, over the front door, was a small cantilevered balcony from which potted plants trailed vines.

Inside, she took a needed breath, her age sometimes a burden, her memories an added weight. She moved slowly through a sitting room and past a cabinet, where photograph albums embalmed her girlhood and her long married life. Occasionally she thumbed through them, fascinated and dismayed by the way the camera had recorded with such exactitude the fading of her beauty and the decline of her husband's health.

In the kitchen she dropped her gloves on the bare table and savored breezes from the ceiling fan. After slaking her thirst with tap water, she slipped off her hot tennis shoes and left humid prints on the parquet. In the bathroom she counted her toes and came up short. Her eyes were not focusing well. She recounted and came up over, aggravating for someone who had spent the greater part of her life teaching high school math.

A shower only half refreshed her. In need of a nap, she climbed the stairs to her bedroom and

4

stretched out on the bed, where she and her husband had enjoyed reading together, she with her mysteries, he with his Dickens. Or his Fielding. He had loved the old masters. She adored Agatha.

Sleep came easily. A vivid dream reunited her with her husband, though shortness of sight kept her from recognizing him until they drew close. They were on a hill, where daytime suddenly transmuted into night. She gazed at stars while he, his back to her, took an urgent leak. "Where have you been?" she asked, and he replied, "Nowhere in particular."

She was unsure how long she had napped, perhaps an hour at the most. Wearing a robe, her feet still bare, she descended the stairs and felt a draft from the cellar door, which stood wide open. From the tail of her eye she glimpsed roses on the kitchen table, a great bouquet of the brightest red from the garden, the thorns enormous on the slashed stems. Behind her came a voice.

"They're for you."

She pivoted. "What are you doing in my house, Bobby?"

Head bent, Trish Becker mounted a bathroom scale as if it were a plinth. Numbers shot crazily from side to side and finally settled. Hands on her bare hips, she gave a backward look into the dim bedroom, where shades were pulled against the late afternoon heat. She said, "You'd tell me if I was too fat, wouldn't you?"

Harry Sawhill, sipping a vodka tonic, smiled from the propped pillows of the bed. "Of course."

She rejoined him on the bed with a drink of her own. She was a close friend and a frequent visitor. Comfortable with her company, he dropped a hand on the marked moon of her abdomen. She was blond, buxom, and jolly. Much in life had become a joke to her, even orgasms. Some women cried after the throes. She laughed.

"Are you going to marry me, Harry?"

"Ask me when I've had a couple more drinks. I'll probably say yes."

Neither was serious. Neither wanted the full-time responsibility of the other. Each had the air of a convalescent. His hand traced over ridges from a caesarean, an appendectomy, a gall bladder removal. Her map of Massachusetts, she had once quipped.

She said, "Let's go to Montreal this weekend."

"Why?" he asked without interest. The thought of travel tired him. At fifty-two, he had a gray look, like late November.

"For the hell of it, Harry. We can do what we want, can't we?"

Each had financial freedom. Trish lived off a generous divorce settlement, and he shared family money with his brother, who, though younger, was his adviser, his mentor, occasionally his savior.

He said, "Get me another drink."

"Take mine, I've had enough." He was the drunk, she was the sport. A sound from downstairs startled her. "What's that?"

"Bobby's home."

"Damn," she said.

"He won't come up. He knows you're here."

Unconvinced, she tossed her legs over the bed's edge and sought her clothing. Dressed, she took out her lipstick and drew a new mouth without looking in a mirror. Her voice had a fullness.

"Why doesn't he like me, Harry?"

"You're not his mother."

His mother had dressed him in yellow and called him a butterball. He was blue eyes squirting out of a face good enough to eat, that was what she told him. Her kisses were nibbles.

He was four years old when she went into the hospital for tests. Though she was gone only three days, her absence tore at him. Her second stay in the hospital stretched to a week, which he saw as a betrayal, for she had promised never to leave him again. The third time she went away she did not return. His father said she had gone to a better place and took him to a large white house, into the cloying scent of cut flowers, where he saw her lying in what seemed a huge basket. He thought she was alive and, overjoyed, tried to climb in. The hands grappling with him belonged to his father and his uncle. His strength surprised them.

"You never should have brought him," his uncle said.

He went to stay with his uncle, whose wife carried the smell of babies. She had twin girls who, despite the help of a nanny, consumed much of her time, leaving little for him. He ate sweets on the sly, which rounded his face. Occasionally he watched the babies being changed. With their legs open, they looked broken, an observation that went uncorrected by the young nanny, who spoke with an accent and may not have understood him.

For his birthday his uncle gave him a singing canary, white with a gray crest, and hung the cage from a kitchen rafter where the cat couldn't get at it. Had he been taller and braver, he'd have freed the bird. Evenings, his uncle usually took him places, to Wenson's Ice Cream Stand, to Burger King, once to a band concert on the green, where he was introduced to the police chief, who was dressed like everyone else, wore no badge, and carried no gun. Patting his head, the chief said, "Anybody gives you trouble, you call me."

"My uncle won't let me go home," he said.

He went home at the end of the month with the caged canary and the full expectation of seeing his mother. He thought he heard her footsteps, but they came from an elderly woman brought in to look after him during the day. His father, liquor on his breath and grief in his eyes, said, "Welcome back."

The woman said, "I like the little birdie. What's his name?"

He placed the cage on a table. "He doesn't have a name. He wants to be free." Then he asked when his mother was coming home, whether she was back at the hospital or still in that big white house.

The woman looked at his father for guidance.

His father, who had been staring into space, suddenly stepped to the cage, opened the little wire door, and reached inside.

"Do you know what dead is, Bobby?" He caught the fluttering canary and crushed it in his hand. "That's what dead is."

Mrs. Bullard was dead. Her body, long limbs askew, lay at the foot of the cellar stairs like a toy to be spun. A single rose lay in the spill of blood. Sergeant Eugene Avery, a veteran of the Bensington Police Department, had a problem staying calm. The sight of unnatural death invariably unsettled his stomach.

"She was a nice lady," he said.

Chief James Morgan, careful of where he stepped, was at the bottom of the stairs. Sergeant Avery remained at the top. Years ago he and the chief had been students of Mrs. Bullard's at the regional high school, where she had been a hard marker but had done her best to pass everyone, though she nearly excluded him. He pricked an ear.

"Did you say something, Chief?"

"Talking to myself." Chief Morgan was a lean shadow in the light of a bare bulb. "What's one rose doing down here? The rest are on the table."

Sergeant Avery thought for a moment. "Maybe she was wearing it in her hair."

"I'm thinking out loud, Eugene."

"I know, but I feel I should answer."

"Looks as if she came down headfirst. With force. Almost as if she were pushed."

9

Sergeant Avery stared down in disbelief. "No signs of a burglary or anything, Chief. You don't think Amy White . . . ?"

"No, that doesn't fly."

Amy White, a friend of Sergeant Avery's sister, looked in on her aunt each evening. Her call to the station had been hysterical. The ambulance that came for her aunt took her away instead.

The chief, who had a woman waiting for him, glanced at his watch. "You got your camera with you? We at least ought to take some pictures."

Dreading the moment, Sergeant Avery descended the stairs with care. Poised over the remains of his former teacher, he felt an inner jolt. Something coming up. He held it back. The chief gave him a quick look and asked if he was all right. Voiceless, tasting himself, he nodded and began working the camera.

"Do you know what bothers me the most, Eugene? That damn rose."

The town's weekly, *The Crier*, which went to press on Wednesday and came out on Thursday, reported that Eve (Perkins) Bullard, 80, a lifelong resident, died Tuesday of injuries from an apparent fall at her home on Grove Street. Arrangements were to be announced by Drinkwater Funeral Home.

Chief Morgan discreetly questioned neighbors and came up dry. A partial autopsy was performed at the general hospital in nearby Lawrence. Mrs. Bullard had succumbed to head trauma, presumably from a fall.

The Bensington Garden Club, of which Mrs. Bullard had been a longtime member and a past president, arranged the flowers at the wake. The Reverend Mr. Austin Stottle of First Congregational Church said prayers.

There was no burial. Mrs. Bullard had willed her body to University Hospital in Boston.

CHAPTER TWO

The days sobered into autumn, and soon it was November, like March a mongrel month, unloved, unloving. The sky was skeletal, schematic, plucked by a crow. The gray in the air only lightly colored Chief Morgan's mood. The chief, whose wife had died young, the victim of a car crash, had learned long ago to take each day at a time and to seek no meaning in the incoherence of grief. As the days shortened, he geared himself to face another winter without a woman. The one he'd been seeing was breaking off with him.

He spent considerable time at a window table in the Blue Bonnet restaurant, which was neatly nestled between the town hall and the library. The window table overlooked the green and all the little shops on the far side. At the flanks were Pearl's Pharmacy and Tuck's General Store. More and more of Tuck's was taking on the look of a superette, displeasing to Morgan. He remembered the waning days of a cracker barrel and penny candy.

At Pearl's he remembered when condoms were called prophylactics and never openly displayed.

His tablemate at breakfast was usually Chub Tuttle from the fire station or Fred Fossey, the part-time veterans agent, whose greatest joy was raising and lowering the flag on the green, Boy Scouts in partial uniform snapping off salutes. At lunch he was frequently joined by Reverend Stottle, who held the private opinion that when God made the human race he got it wrong but won't admit his mistake. The chief, though not a churchgoer, was among those with whom the reverend shared confidences, which included his weakness for unapproachable women in his congregation, those hefty in the thigh and overblown with goodness.

Crossing the green with the reverend, Morgan bumped into Amy White, who said she was putting her aunt's house on the market. Positioning her back to the wind, which had teeth, she said she couldn't bear to step foot through that door again. The chief told her it was a tough time to sell and advised her to wait until spring.

"We've priced it to move," she said and gave Reverend Stottle a haggard look. "I can still see her lying at the foot of those cellar stairs. Do you think she's at peace?"

"Death," said Reverend Stottle, "is winter without storms."

Harry Sawhill needed a nip in the morning to get him going and another at noon to keep him smiling. At night the drinking turned serious and put him to

14

sleep. Trish Becker, who saw him two or three times a week, said, "You can't go on this way."

He said, "It's the only way I know."

They were in Andover, in the bar at Rembrandt's, a restaurant off the square. Their table was tiny, and they sat knee to knee. Trish was drinking a martini and picking at peanuts. "If I had your balls in my hand," she said, "would you trust me not to squeeze?"

He thought for a moment. "Yes, I think so."

"Then trust me now. You need help."

Moments later she rose from the table in her thigh-high dress and, heading toward the ladies' room, drew looks from men at the bar, none of whom interested her, all of the sort who make vague passes but lack confidence to execute direct ones. Alone in the ladies' room, she compressed her lips and viewed herself in the mirror. "Beauty's mortal, my dear," she murmured aloud. "Be careful." Then she dabbed her hot face with a damp tissue and hoped she wasn't going through the change.

She returned to the table. Harry, nursing his vodka tonic, gave her a half smile. There were moments when they seemed to see into each other. He said, "I'm going to try."

She glanced at the men at the bar. Most appeared placid and uncomplicated, with skim-milk complexions, no five o'clock shadows. "Try what, Harry?"

"To get myself together."

She drove her fingers into the peanuts. "No, Harry. No, you won't."

15

* * *

Trish Becker lived in the Heights, home to Bensington's well-heeled newcomers. Once an expanse of pristine woodland, it was now a meandering avenue of grand houses. Ben Sawhill also lived there, the only townie who did. It was too late for a phone call, but she rang his number anyway.

"Belle's in bed," he said.

"I want to talk to you." He was her lawyer, her financial adviser, her confidant, and his wife Belle was her buddy. "I hate my house."

"What's the matter with it?"

"Everything," she said. The house was an elegant red-brick Georgian with a wing for guests. Since her divorce it had quietly assumed a personality she didn't care for. Some rooms, no matter how warm the colors, had a chilling effect, as if they held grudges. The kitchen, which should have been friendly with its great bow window, seemed menacing, perhaps because of the many utensils hanging from ceiling racks. The dining room, the windows heavily draped, seemed disengaged from the rest of the house.

"I told you to sell it four years ago," he said.

"The market wasn't right. You said so yourself."

"You heard what you wanted to hear. What's really wrong, Trish? It isn't the house."

She shifted her cordless phone from one hand to the other and flung her hair back. Her feet were shod in fleece-lined slippers. "I hate November," she said.

"It's not a pleasant month. So what?" He waited a moment, then added, "This isn't like you."

"That's because your brother's turning me into a drunk. It's your fault. You introduced us—you and Belle."

"We thought it was a good idea at the time."

"He's a dead end. And I'm Dorothy Parker's big blonde, that's what I am."

"Dorothy Parker's blonde had no money. You do. That's all the difference in the world." His voice was sharp, authoritative. "And you have children."

She had a son in college and a daughter in boarding school, their holidays spent with their father, who had remarried and was said to wear his new young wife on his arm for fashion, as if she'd come out of his wardrobe. The last she had seen of him was in *Newsweek,* a picture of him in a designer suit and color-splashed tie, his executive abilities lauded, his software company touted.

"You don't understand," she said. "I was a good wife."

Ben was quiet. She imagined dark tones in his face. Her mind's eye saw the prominence of his jaw, a striking feature he shared with Harry, as if they'd been line-bred for it. She wondered whether Belle was waiting for him.

"Still there?" she asked.

"You're right, Trish. November's a lousy month."

"Don't tell Harry I called."

17

"I wouldn't dream of it."

"Don't tell Belle either," she said.

Bobby Sawhill stared out of his bedroom window at leafless trees that reminded him of empty bird-cages. The stillness of the trees and the pallor of the sky affected his thoughts. It was his birthday. He was a November baby.

He heard footsteps on the stairs and turned from the window. His room was neat, everything in place, nothing on the walls, no posters, no heroes. No stereo. Stereo music hurt his head. A computer given to him by his uncle did not interest him. He kept the television on but seldom watched. Girlie magazines interested him, but the theater in his head interested him more. He preferred the past to the present, skits in which he was barefoot, his toes grass-stained, his mother counting them. This little piggy went to market, this little piggy . . .

His father rapped on the door and opened it. "We leave at six. That all right?"

He remembered a neighbor woman catching sight of him with his pants down, calling his little thing a bullet, and telling him it'd be awhile before he fired it.

"Did you hear me, Bobby?"

He consulted his watch and shrugged. It was four o'clock, which made six o'clock a long time off.

"We can make it earlier or later," his father said, "whatever you wish."

It didn't matter.

When he heard the door close he gathered up schoolbooks and planted himself at his writing table. He did only what he had to in homework, which came easy to him. School did not. Where others sought attention he avoided it. Teachers overlooked his long silences because his grades were adequate and his father was somebody. He had no friends.

A few minutes before six his father called to him. Descending the stairs, he glimpsed Trish Becker and whispered, "Why does she have to come?"

On the drive to Andover he sat in the back and Trish Becker sat beside his father, who fought the feral glare of oncoming headlights. Screwing her head around, Trish Becker said, "Wow, you're thirteen now. A teenager."

"It's no big deal," he said.

At Rembrandt's they were ushered through the lounge and shown to a choice table on the glassed-in porch. The waitress brought aperitifs. He was given a glass of ginger ale topped with crushed ice, through which he punched a straw. Trish Becker smiled at him. She wore eyeliner and showed cleavage. Her hand came forward in the suggestion of a touch and fell back when he said, "I'd like my presents now."

"After dinner when the cake comes," his father said.

"I don't want a cake."

Trish Becker's gift was a Cross pen, which did not impress him, though he mumbled a thank-you. His father's gift pleased him less.

19

"I already have a watch."

"You have a Timex," his father said. "This is a Seiko."

"You have a Rolex."

"You'll get one when you graduate from high school."

Menus were read. When the waitress came for their orders, he said, "I'll have pizza."

"They don't have pizza," his father said. "Order something real."

He ordered what they did, poached salmon. He ate only the edges. His father finished first and ordered a vodka tonic; then excused himself and went to the men's room. Left alone with Trish Becker, Bobby read sympathy in her eyes and disliked her for it. She reached under the table and placed a hand on his knee.

"Do we need to be enemies?"

His face was passive, his voice cool. "Are you going to marry my father?"

She spoke slowly. "Would it upset you if I did?"

"I wouldn't like it."

"Chances are I won't," she said. "Why are you staring at me like that?"

"I know what you look like naked. I've seen pictures."

She was confused, somewhat shocked. "Of me, Bobby?"

"Other women."

Something clicked, and she seemed on the point of laughter as if from an image of his face slammed into a double issue of *Penthouse*. "I'm flattered, Bobby."

"Why?"

"Just am."

His father returned. In time the cake he didn't want came anyway, with candles he was obliged to blow out. Trish Becker sliced three neat pieces, the biggest for him, more frosting than the others. Her smile was knowing.

"Happy birthday, Bobby."

Winter came early with a heavy snowfall of dry furry flakes. In the light of morning, the storm spent, Chief Morgan shoveled his walk and knocked snow from arborvitae, which instantly diffused a fresh green aroma. He cleared enough of the short driveway to get his car out of the garage. The car, public property, unmarked except for the fading town seal, stuttered before it found a voice and stalled only once on the plowed street.

The police station, situated in a rear corner of the town hall, the entrance on the side, was just large enough to accommodate the ten-member force, which included the chief and three civilian dispatchers. Meg O'Brien, the daytime dispatcher, gave him a penetrating look when he pushed through the door. He stamped snow from thick-soled shoes and shed his gloves but kept on his parka.

"You have problems," Meg said. "One of the cruisers broke down, and Eugene ran the other into a snowbank."

"Those aren't problems, they're aggravations."
He was anxious to slip over to the Blue Bonnet for
breakfast, but Meg's gaze held him. Big eyes and
heavy teeth overwhelmed her pony face. A bond of
affection existed between them, though occasionally she got on his nerves. "Anything else?"

"Claudia MacLeod wants you to call her. I
thought you two broke up again."

"Did I tell you that?"

"You didn't have to. She's a good woman, Jim,
not like some of those tootsies you've played
around with."

His past relationships with a couple of high-
strung women from the Heights had distressed
her, but his association with Claudia MacLeod, a
shaky romance at best, on-again, off-again, pleased
her. Claudia was a townie.

"Have I ever told you to mind your own business?"

"Many times. Think about something, Jim. With
her you know what you're getting."

Claudia Perrault, her name back then, had been
his eighth-grade girlfriend. They had walked hand-
in-hand in the woods girding Paget's Pond. Their
initials, carved into the juicy skin of a sugar maple,
had long ago been sucked into the heartwood.

Meg gentled her tone. "You've both had your
tragedies."

Claudia had married young and followed her
soldier husband to Georgia, where she waited for
him after he was sent to Vietnam. He was killed in
a final round of fighting. She returned to Bensing-

ton with his partial remains, buried them in Burnham Road Cemetery, and moved in with her widowed mother, a household that now included her two aunts.

Meg said, "You could be more understanding."

"Everybody could be that, Meg. Everybody in the world."

"But we're talking about you. You're not getting any younger. None of us are."

He was in his forties, and Meg, who had never married, was past fifty. Her concerns were him, her job, and her cats. She had no living relatives. Her closest brush with romance was in a doctor's office when she was a young woman. A professional hand searching for her pain momentarily turned affectionate, a horror to her then, not altogether a bad memory now.

Morgan unzipped his parka. "Is she home?"

"She's at work."

He entered an office not quite small enough to cramp him and, bulky in his open parka, sat at his desk. A photograph of his wife stood beside his calendar pad and telephone. He rang up Claudia at the regional high school, where she was a guidance counselor. They talked for several minutes, quietly, businesslike, the subject surprising to him. Meg crept in with a mug of coffee for him and tiptoed out. In a low voice, he said, "I don't understand. You could move in with me."

Claudia's voice was lower. "I need to have my own place. My own life."

The conversation ended a few moments later.

He wrapped his hands around the coffee mug, which had a blue-and-gold pattern and was the sole survivor of a set given him ten years ago when he was appointed chief. Meg looked in on him.

He said, "She wants to buy the Bullard house."

During the afternoon the temperature plunged, and by nightfall the cold was bitter. Returning home, Chief Morgan raised the heat and heard the furnace kick in under his feet. He disliked the dark and soon had light pouring through every downstairs room. Wind rattled windows. The house, old and ill-insulated, had belonged to his parents. He and his wife had planned to rejuvenate it, add on a room. In the framework of the future, the house had seemed tiny. Now it echoed.

Claudia MacLeod arrived at seven with take-out from the Blue Bonnet and an overnight bag. Chicken wings, mashed potatoes, gravy, cranberry sauce, and rolls were in the take-out. Among other things, flannel pajamas jammed the overnight bag.

"I didn't think you'd come," he said, for she was an infrequent visitor and seldom stayed the night.

"Are you glad?"

"I'm grateful," he said nakedly. Women were important to him. Female presence was a weapon against the void in a way that male companionship never could be. "What about your mother?"

"I'm a big girl, James."

Setting plates on the kitchen table, he watched her open hot containers and sniff aromas. Her hair, light brown, free of gray, was parted in the middle. Her eyes were wistful and inquiring behind sober spectacles and often ambiguous about what they wanted. Dowdy in clothes, purposely so, she was the opposite otherwise.

"What if your mother needs you?"

"Don't push it, James."

He placed salt and pepper on the table. "Sorry."

Her mother and her aunts, a sore subject between them, didn't want him taking her away from them. They competed with him and each other for her time and attention. In an airless world of their own making, they depended on her to attend to their wants, referee their squabbles, and run their errands.

"Milk?"

"Please," she said.

They ate quietly, at ease with each other, her company a wave of warmth for him. Chewing, she caught him staring.

"Like an old married couple, aren't we?" she said.

"Not exactly."

She frowned slightly. "Do you understand why I want to buy the Bullard place?"

He understood that her mother's house, only a little larger than his, had the closeness of a sickroom and the telltale odor of shut-ins. Her aunts, who vied over whose grief from widowhood was greater, never went out unless she packed them in her Dodge Colt and drove them. Her mother lived with the constant fear of chills.

"I know the obvious reasons," he said. "Maybe there are some I don't know. Or don't want to know."

"I'm living in the past, James. I can't go on doing that." She buttered a roll and handed it to him. "Sometimes I think I'm regressing. I don't want to take care of my mother. I want her to take care of me."

"More gravy?"

"No, you finish it," she said. "Everything OK?"

"Everything's fine."

"When I was a child I loved wetting my pants. It was wicked but felt good. And someone was always there to scold me, lovingly of course." Abruptly she laughed, her glasses refracting light. "I can't believe I told you that."

"But you did."

She wiped her mouth. "I'm a dunce."

He had a dishwasher, but it was broken. He did the dishes in the sink, and she dried them. Reaching into a cupboard to put away her milk glass, she glimpsed a June bug reduced to its shell. Telephone numbers were penciled on the inside of the cupboard door, hers among them. Below, near the toaster, the paper toweling was down to its cylinder, which bore shreds of the last sheet.

"You need someone to look after you, James?"

"Want the job?"

"I have a small life, room only for me."

Later, in another room, magazines and newspapers strewn about, they watched television from separate cushioned chairs. She sat with her legs curled under her, her cardigan pulled tight. Her eyes were more on him than the screen. His had closed.

26

"Do you want to share your thoughts," she asked, "or do you prefer to think alone?"

"I thought you were watching the program."

"No more than you are." When his eyes opened, she said, "In some ways you remind me of my father. That disturbs me."

"I remember he was a nice fellow. So it shouldn't disturb you."

"A week after he died my mother washed his underwear and socks, folded them how she always did, and placed them neatly in his dresser drawer as if he were coming back."

Morgan gripped the armrests of his chair. "I'm not interested in television, are you?"

"No," she said.

They climbed the stairs. In his bedroom he closed the door behind them and partly raised a window which let in the cold and the howl of the wind. He watched her hurry into a pajama top. She had a fine bottom, two perfect bowls. His sleepwear was a gray sweatshirt. Before getting into bed, he threw an extra blanket over the bed. In the growing warmth under the covers they lay close together.

"My father whistled his own tune," she said, "never anybody else's."

"I do the same, though off-key."

"I've noticed."

Deep under the covers they made love. He loved the business of it. Two humid bodies impacting, his driving home messages and hers wallowing in the words. Vainly he tried to make it last. When he

27

started to withdraw, she rose under him, gripped him with arms and legs, and held him fixed.

Later, when he thought she was drifting off to sleep, he said, "I know you love me."

"But if I don't have you, I can't lose you."

"You'd never lose me, Claudia," he said and in the dark sensed her turning her face away.

"I don't trust you, James. You might leave me."

"No."

"Yes," she said. "You might die."

Trish Becker, who despised winter, wanted the warmth of the Caribbean. "Let's take a cruise on a gambling ship, Harry. I love the slots. I love black-jack, don't you?"

Harry Sawhill shook his head. He enjoyed win-ning of course, he said, but losing was a silly way to part with money.

"But there's a thrill to the game," she said.

"French kissing gives me a thrill, gambling doesn't."

"You could lick the chips."

Harry glared. They were dinner guests of his brother and sister-in-law, the four of them seated in ameliorating candlelight. Belle Sawhill, who had soft engaging features and a richly intimate voice, said, "It's a joke, Harry."

Trish was seated beside Ben Sawhill, which pleased her. She liked Ben's clipped correctness, admired his successes, and envied his wife. He wore a Rolex with the face under his wrist, which reminded her of a gunfighter sporting his six-shooter with the handle pointed out.

He said to her, "Winter wouldn't be so bad for you if you skied."

"I love the lodges, Ben, not the slopes."

Harry complimented Belle for the second time on the superb taste of the seared swordfish, which was blackened with Cajun sauce. The wine, his brother's choice, was an expensive *Graves,* Belle said to him, "How's Bobby?"

"He's all right. He's fine."

"No, he's not," Trish said.

Harry spoke low across the table. "Not your business."

"He's never been right," Ben said gently. "Not since his mother died."

"I do my best."

Belle touched his arm. "We know you do."

After dessert, they retired to the library, where a fire was going. Belle served coffee, a choice of decaf and regular. The twins, who had stayed up past their bedtime, came in to say good night. Sammantha and Jennifer were healthy nine-year-olds, the blood glistening through their skin. They had Belle's black hair, dark eyes, and full mouth. Trish gave hugs to each and said, "I still can't tell you two apart."

"I'm Jennifer," Sammantha said.

"No, she's not," said Jennifer. "I am!"

Sammantha was independent, contrary, and Jennifer was the darling. They competed for affection from their father, who adored them both, no apparent favorite. Belle said, "Say good night to your uncle."

They kissed Harry's cheek and gave smackers to their father. Their nanny, who had been waiting in the doorway, took them off to bed. Ben and Harry slipped away to talk business, Harry's personal finances, the state of his investments. Belle and Trish remained by the fire with their coffee.

"The twins are lovely," Trish said.

"I don't know what I'd do without them."

"Didn't you want another child or two?"

"It wasn't possible."

"I'm sorry, I didn't know. Still, you're very lucky."

"Yes, I think so."

"Is Ben a good lover?"

For an instant Belle was taken aback. "I have no complaints."

"Harry isn't. He drinks too much, and it stunts his performance. When he's at his best I pretend he's Ben."

Belle looked into the fire. "I wish you hadn't told me that."

"It's nothing serious, only fantasy. Besides, what would Ben want with a broad like me?"

When the brothers returned, Harry was smiling, a celebratory drink in his hand. "Guess what," he said to Trish, "I'm richer than I thought."

In the middle of January Trish Becker had had enough of winter. Waking early and unable to fall back to sleep, she rose from her king-sized bed, parted window drapes, and looked out at a fierce boreal dawn. The sun, a lump of white, looked frozen. "To hell with this," she said aloud and made plans. At noontime she phoned an old friend, Gloria Eisner, who lived in Connecticut and told her what she had in mind for the two of them.

"For how long?" Gloria asked.

"A month. How 'bout it?"

Three days later she and Gloria were sunbathing on a Barbados beach. Gloria lay prone on a towel with her head cradled in her arms and her eyes gazing out over the curve of a well-oiled shoulder. Trish, her face wrapped in sunglasses, sat in a chaise and sipped rum punch. Ten feet away a man with protruding eyes, like push buttons, stood sour, sandy, touched by too much sun. He stared intently at them before moving on. Half under her breath, Trish said, "What are we, freaks?"

"He was looking at your breasts," Gloria said. "They've always been a big deal."

"He was looking at my belly scars."

Best friends in high school, they had been the sort boys orbited. Inseparable, they had frequently slept over at each other's house. In bed they had compared their breasts and the maturity between their legs. Trish had the bigger bosom, Gloria the richer pubes. Each had married right out of college. Gloria had had three husbands, Trish only the one.

"Seeing anyone special?" Trish asked.

Gloria stretched a lengthy leg and dug her toe in

the sand. "A few guys, no music in any of them. You still seeing that same man? What's his name?"

"Harry. I'm thinking of breaking it off. No future."

"Don't you know what the future is, Trish? It's today squeezed into tomorrow. My last husband told me that."

Sipping her punch, Trish watched a wave flop in. The sea was full of wrinkles and smiles. "All I know is that as you grow older things become less solid. Houses, relationships, dreams."

"Tell me about it."

Trish put the punch glass aside and rose from the chaise. A bikini clung bravely to her full showy body. Hands on her hips, she looked down at Gloria. "Tell me the truth. Do I look ridiculous?"

"You're big in the bust, you can't help that. No, you don't look ridiculous. You look beautiful."

Wearing straw hats and open silk shirts, they strolled the beach. Waves were coming in green now. A fishing boat plowed a path toward deep waters. They passed a child whispering into a shell, a man slipping on a frog mask, young women scampering into the surf.

"You ever scared, Gloria?"

"Of what? Dying?"

"Living, aging, all that stuff."

Gloria tossed her a big smile. "Every minute of the day."

Escaping the relentless sun, they browsed a seafront shop that sold scrimshaw, shells, driftwood, and watercolors of tropical storms. Tired, thirsty, they returned to the hotel and had drinks at the veranda bar, where a man who looked extremely clean, perhaps because he was bald and wore white, bought them a round.

He had a British accent, a slight stammer, and a chin line no longer firm. When he placed a hand on Trish's knee, she said, "Give me a break!"

He soon left.

"You looking to get laid, Gloria?"

"I could've stayed home for that."

"Good. Because I'm not either."

Gloria's drink was exotic, and she licked sugar from her lips. "Unless of course someone scrumptious comes along."

"That's different."

They napped for an hour in their room, then showered and dressed. Her chestnut hair tied with a ribbon, Gloria looked defiantly slender and poignantly attractive in a brief evening dress. In the same cut of garment, Trish appeared dewy, bouncy, spontaneous. She dabbed a touch of Gloria's perfume on her wrist. They dined in the smaller of the hotel's two restaurants, at a table marked by elegant linen and muted by candle glow. The offerings of a harpist made Trish think of tinkling water drops and Grecian rockscape.

"You've been to Greece, haven't you, Gloria?"

"Twice. Once on my honeymoon, I forget which husband."

"Three failed marriages, Gloria. Does that ever depress you?"

"I take it philosophically. Every song plays itself out."

Trish finished feasting on turtle steaks, which she had a taste for. Gloria consumed a fried fillet of grouper. Declining dessert and coffee, they ordered after-dinner drinks, which arrived promptly. Trish's was redolent of rose petals and cloves.

"Don't let me get tight."

"Why not?" Gloria said. "You can do what you want here."

"I'll get maudlin. The holidays did a number on me. The kids spent them with their father, of course. He's the one broke up the marriage, but they still blame me for it."

"Fathers do no wrong. Mothers are bitches."

"Where's it written?"

"God's male. He wrote it."

They sipped their liqueurs slowly and then called for the check. Trish signed it and wrote in a generous gratuity. Gloria left a little something for the harpist. They wandered through the lobby and out into the soft night. The sky over the sea was immense and aggressively bright with stars. Gloria said, "Do you remember my second husband?"

Trish tended to remember voices. She remembered his. Deep and authoritative.

"He wore power suspenders, cardinal red," Gloria said. "Making money and making underlings jump was what he was all about. He thought he could make *me* jump."

Trish remembered dining with them at Locke-Ober's. When a gold crown fell into his lobster pie, she thought it was a cuff link. "How did you do in the settlement?"

34

.

"He had the better lawyer."

Dropping her head back, Trish gazed up at the glittering immensity of the sky. Her voice had a tremor. "The eye deceives," she said. "The spaces between the stars look manageable."

"But we know otherwise," Gloria said.

When they returned to their room, Trish placed a call to Harry Sawhill. His son answered. Gloria slipped into the bathroom and used the john. At the sink, the tap running, she sniffed and then used a small oval of pastel green soap, which in her wet hands produced a plethora of rich and dainty suds. She brushed her teeth and with another brush, with softer bristles, massaged her gums. When she emerged from the bathroom, Trish was sitting on the edge of one of the beds.

"What's wrong?"

"Harry says he misses me."

"That's wonderful."

"His kid says he hates me."

"You're going to hear from my mother," Claudia MacLeod warned Chief Morgan, and he soon did. On a January morning so cold it seemed inconceivable that it would ever be warm again, he drove to Mrs. Perrault's Spring Street house, where an abundance of utility lines raced from the street to an eave of the roof. Swiftly ushered in, he was seated in an armchair than seemed to remember him, though he had never sat in it before. The thermostat pushed to the limit, the room throbbed with arid heat. Mrs. Perrault and her two older sisters, all swathed in heavy sweaters, shared the sofa.

"Is she doing the right thing, James?"

Mrs. Perrault had known him since he was a child. He had delivered her newspaper. He had slipped a valentine for Claudia through the mail slot. For a dollar he had mowed their lawn. He said, "I'm not sure."

"Of course she isn't!" the elder sister snapped.

"Her home is here," said the other sister.

Both had ghost-white hair that revealed the fine pink of their scalps. The veiny tops of their hands looked inlaid with mother-of-pearl. The elder sister had the larger presence, the greater voice.

"What does she want to live alone for?"

"Please, Ida," Mrs. Perrault said. "Let James speak."

"I think Claudia's doing what she wants to do," Morgan said gently. "She wants to be on her own."

Mrs. Perrault gazed at him with mournful eyes. The dyes in her tightly permed hair were of conflicting hues. "But nobody wants to live alone."

Morgan wanted to say that Claudia was tired of being answerable to their moods. He wanted to say that a woman in her forties deserves independence. He said nothing.

"Isn't she happy here, James?"

"That's not the point."

A harsh voice said, "There is no point."

"Ida, please."

Ida's large painted mouth clenched into a red fist. The eyes of the other sister were rapid blinks.

Mrs. Perrault, who had been the baby of the family, bore no resemblance to either of them, which years ago had given credence to gossip that their mother's passions had stretched beyond the marriage bed.

"We didn't ask if you wanted coffee, James."

"Well, *ask* him," said Ida.

"I have to get back," Morgan said, rising.

Accompanying him to the door, Mrs. Perrault seemed to move on tiptoe, on air. The hues in her hair sparkled, as if her head held explosives. At the door, as he zipped his parka and hiked the collar, she touched his arm.

"You have to do something, James."

"What should I do?"

"Marry her."

Morgan looked at her critically. "That's a switch, isn't it?"

"Better she have someone than no one."

Amy White accepted Claudia MacLeod's second offer for Mrs. Bullard's house, which included the furniture and all of the books. Eyes filling, Amy said, "I'm glad it's you, Claudia, and not some out-of-towner buying the place. Auntie Eve would be pleased."

A week later, the third day of a January thaw, Chief Morgan investigated a break-in at the unoccupied house. The intruder forced an entry through the bulkhead and tracked mud up the cellar steps and through the house. As far as Amy could determine, nothing had been taken or disturbed, though it seemed to Morgan that someone had lain on Mrs. Bullard's bed, the same someone who probably had left the toilet seat up.

Dining with Claudia at Rembrandt's that evening in Andover, Morgan said, "It's not too late to back out. I mean, if you have any doubts."

"Now you sound like my mother."

"She thinks we should get married."

Claudia sipped her wine, her second refill. "Yes, she told me."

"Maybe you should think about it."

"I have, a great deal," she said softly. "I could never marry a policeman. It'd be like marrying a soldier again. I couldn't bear that."

He was surprised. It was the first time in years that she had mentioned her husband. A Bensington boy. Among the first to enlist from their graduating class, his name now engraved on the war memorial outside the library and on the formidable one in Washington. Morgan said, "I was a soldier too."

"But you came back."

In Vietnam he had served with hillbillies from Kentucky and Tennessee, their bravery astonishing, foolhardy. So many had died. So many had volunteered for second tours.

"All these years gone by, James, I still miss him."

They were, he suspected, subject to the same sense of loss and emptiness, to the same attacks of loneliness, to the same surges of panic. "A day doesn't go by that I don't think of my wife."

"Are they somewhere else, or are we just kidding ourselves?"

"There's the mystery."

"Yes, there's the rub."

The waitress took away dishes and returned with coffee. Candlelight caught Claudia's glasses and wouldn't let go. Morgan gazed through the glare, his emotions warm. He was well aware that other men considered her plain, distant, bloodless, but they had never seen her in the round, never felt her tongue in their ear, never shared her moments of passion. Drinking his coffee, he enjoyed the silence between them.

"Let me," she said when the check came.

"Absolutely not," he said, producing a credit card. "This is a celebration. You're changing your life."

"For the better, James?"

"We'll see."

Outside the cloakroom he held her coat, and she crippled her arms into the sleeves. Brushing aside her hair, he kissed the back of her neck.

"I love you, Claudia."

"I love you too, James."

Trish Becker returned from the Caribbean in the final week of February. Harry Sawhill was waiting for her at Logan Airport and, bolting toward her, threw his arms around her. "Wow," she said, "I'll have to do this more often."

"Don't ever go away that long again." He looked

hangdog. "You don't know how much I missed you."

"You can tell me later."

Moving through the milling crowd to pick up her luggage, he said, "I don't know what I'd do if anything happened to you."

"What could happen?"

The drive to the cold stillness, shocked trees, and winter-bleached grass of Bensington took forty minutes. They drove to the Heights, her big brick house waiting for her, though she was not truly glad to be back. Had it been April or May, she might have been. Harry, who had kept an eye on the house for her, carried the luggage in.

"Home sweet home," she said tightly.

"What's the matter?"

"Nothing," she said. "Absolutely nothing."

In the oversized kitchen, the heels of her pumps clicking over octagonal tiles, she prepared to make coffee. Harry drew their favorite mugs from the cabinet. She had cleared out the refrigerator, but he had since stocked it with milk, cheese, eggs, and butter. A loaf of dark rye bread was on the counter.

"Thanks, Harry."

He took his coffee black. In a strained voice, he said, "You have a good time?"

"So much sky down there, Harry, I couldn't help thinking God was keeping an eye on me."

"Meet anyone?"

"No one worth mentioning." She joined him at

the table. Her face was deeply tanned, which made her hair blonder. "Gloria thought we might get in each other's way after a while, but we didn't."

He was quiet. She could tell by his eyes that he had something vital to reveal. On the brink of a smile he said, "I've been sober."

"You're kidding. The whole time?"

He nodded. "I did a lot of thinking while you were gone. I want us to be permanent, Trish."

"Are you proposing?"

"That's what I'm doing."

She took a slow sip of coffee. "What if I say yes? Bobby won't like it."

"I've already talked to him about it. You're right, he's not happy, but he'll come around."

She sighed heavily, as if coping with one too many players in her life. "I've just gotten back, Harry. You're hitting me with too much."

"Is that a no?"

"Give me breathing time."

His hand creeping across the table, he rolled his eyes at the ceiling. "It's been more than a month. What d'you say?"

Together they climbed the wide stairway to the master bedroom, which was shadowy in the dying day. Trish switched on a lamp and stood in its brightness. For a moment she viewed herself in a triptych of mirrors, but then her eye shifted to footprints sullying the carpet.

"Were you up here, Harry?"

"No. Why do you ask?"

"Were you lying on my bed?"

He laughed. "Of course not."

"Someone was," she said.

Two days later, watching the start of a hard snow-fall from a wide window, she phoned Gloria Eisner in Connecticut and said, "What if I told you I'm thinking of getting married?"

There was a slight pause. "To your friend?"

"Yes."

"Then I'd say give it a lot more thought."

She moved closer to the window. The snow was making packages of the evergreens. "I need a life," she said.

"What's wrong with the one you've got?"

"There's nothing in it."

"Do you love him?" Gloria asked after a pause.

"At our age, what does that have to do with it?"

"As long as you're not going from nothing to nothing."

"Who's to say, Gloria? Who's the hell to say?"

Later she phoned Ben Sawhill at his office in Boston and told him what she was considering. Silent for a moment, he cleared his throat and said, "Sounds like a good deal for Harry. Is it for you?"

"It's not a business deal, Ben. It's two human be-ings looking ahead. My concern is Bobby. Do you think he'll be a problem?"

"Isn't he already one?"

The wind sounded like a truck charging the house. Her face to the window, she saw snow gust-ing like heavy smoke. Much had fallen, reshaping shrubs, burdening trees, and cushioning a stone bench. "Really getting bad out there," she said. "Shouldn't you be starting home?"

"I'm staying over. I booked a room at the Ritz."

"Do you want company? I'll drive in."

He was silent. She had known he would be.

"Just joking, Ben." She turned from the window. "I called for advice. Yours means a lot to me."

"Comes down to one thing," he said. "Can you survive another upheaval in your life?"

"No sweat," she said in a reckless voice. "Things don't work out, I'll just say *shazam* and fly away."

In February Amy White and Claudia MacLeod met with their lawyers at the registry of deeds in nearby Lawrence and swiftly passed papers on Mrs. Bullard's house. The lawyers, anxious to move on, snapped their briefcases shut and said good-bye. Pocketing a check, Amy turned to Claudia and said, "It's really yours now. I know you'll be happy in it. My aunt was."

Claudia waited until the mild part of March to move in. Chief Morgan helped her. Standing outside together, they admired the little balcony over the front door. Claudia called it a fairybook house while ignoring the uncertain condition of the roof and the missing slats in one of the shutters. She opened the door for him, and he lugged in a box of her belongings. On the parlor walls were oblong patches where family pictures had hung. In the kitchen waterdrops twitched out of a leaky faucet. From the attic came the scurry of mice.

43

"I know what you're thinking," she said.

He placed the box on a chair. When he opened the cellar door, a draft flew up at him. The light cord was a string tied to a stub of chain. He pulled it and peered down the stairs, more narrow and warped than he'd remembered.

"Is that where she fell, James?"

"That's where it happened," he said.

Without telling her, he replaced the lock on the bulkhead with a heavy-duty one, the best Brody's Hardware had to offer, and placed the key on the kitchen table, a tag identifying it.

"You worry too much," she said.

He kissed her and undid a button on her blouse. When he brushed the back of his hand across the start of her breasts, she shuddered as if he had crept across her grave.

"I do," he said, a chill inside his skull, as if memory, running ahead of itself, were recording what hadn't happened yet. They made love upright, against the cellar door, she with a knee hiked high.

Afterward, he didn't want to let her go. "I wish we had more time," he whispered. "Why can't a second be a minute and a minute an hour? Why can't we hold our breath forever?"

"My back hurts," she said.

In April she hung new curtains in the parlor and gazed out at forsythia gushing into bloom while a naked magnolia tree waited to be clothed. In another window she shaded her eyes from the sun. The promise of daffodils spiked the gray earth of a garden that still looked wretched from winter.

Holding her gaze, fascinating her, was the agile strength of a robin drawing up a worm from the packed ground, stringing it out whole, careful not to break it.

One evening, at Morgan's request, Sergeant Avery arrived unannounced with a battered toolbox and fixed the dripping faucet in the kitchen. When she tried to pay him, he said, "No charge. Chief and I are buddies."

Morgan arrived a little later with pizza and beer and a large smile. He immediately tested the faucet. "Not bad, huh?"

She said, "Let me take care of myself, James."

His feelings were visible on his face. "Don't shut me out."

In May the garden vibrated with colors. Crimson tulips of an exotic variety danced with daffodils among lilies not yet in blossom. Irises floated high over their foliage of knives. Awaiting a wearer was a gown of flowering almond.

In the early light of a Saturday morning the garden was tremulous, vaporous, colors riding over muted green. Claudia was on her knees weeding and listening to birdsong. The loudest was an elaborate trill from a cardinal whose mate was unresponsive. Then she heard a voice halfway between a man's and a child's.

"I knew the lady who lived here before. You her daughter?"

"No." Getting to her feet, she nearly scratched herself on a thorn.

"Those are rose bushes."

"I know," she said. He looked familiar and absurdly young for his size. "What's your name?"

"Bobby," he said.

Meg O'Brien fidgeted at her desk. Her oldest cat was incontinent and needed to be put away, which she could not bring herself to do. Chief Morgan, trying to be helpful, offered Sergeant Avery's services and immediately wished he hadn't. Her pony face tossed high, she said, "I'll take care of my own cat, thank you."

Morgan retired to his office to watch baseball on a miniature TV set. Among the Red Sox players was Crack Alexander, who had bought a house in the Heights and was the town's celebrity. Morgan watched him line the ball to center field, where it was caught at the base of the bleacher wall. Morgan's groan joined that of the crowd.

Meg peered in at him. "Matt just called in sick."

Matt MacGregor, one of his youngest officers, worked the second shift. Without removing his eyes from the little screen, Morgan said, "No problem. I'll be around."

"You got nothing better to do?"

"That's right."

Resettling himself behind his desk, Morgan piddled away an hour watching the Sox lose to the Orioles, the game never close, though Crack Alexander hit a solo home run in the final inning. Rising to stretch his legs, he heard a shrieking horn from a car circling the green. Teenagers. He heard Reverend Stottle ringing the church bell not for a service but for the early start of a bean supper, tickets available at the door. Then he noticed that Meg was back in the doorway.

"Mrs. Perrault says she's been trying to reach Claudia all day. She wants you to go over and check on her."

Morgan sighed. "She's either out in the garden or, more likely, not answering the phone. Her mother calls constantly, not to mention her aunts."

"You're not going over?"

"Send Eugene," he said and drew a frown. Hand on her hip, Meg awaited an explanation, as if she had the rights of an elder sister. He said, "We're not getting along so well."

"What's the matter now, Jim?"

"She thinks I'm too much in her face."

"Are you?"

"Probably. I know she cares for me, but I don't think she loves me."

Meg stared intently. "Would you like a hard truth, Jim? A woman loves only once. After that it's pretense, reenactment, wishful thinking."

He stared back. "How would you know that?"

"I was young once, remember?"

He half smiled. "Is it the same for a man?"

"You tell me," she said and turned away.

Coffee at his elbow, he scanned a newsletter from the Massachusetts Association of Police Chiefs and, with slightly more interest, browsed a magazine article on urban crime. Then he heard

Meg calling to him from her desk. The cadence
went out of his stride when he stepped out of his
office and saw her face. She stood with the telephone receiver down by her side.

"It's Eugene," she said. "Get over there, Jim."

CHAPTER THREE

Trembling, Sergeant Avery said, "I'm sorry, Chief."

Edging into the kitchen, Morgan felt the hair move on his head, and all of a sudden his breathing was choppy. Claudia MacLeod's final moment was frozen on her face.

"You want me to call the state police?"

Morgan lacked a voice, so he nodded. The blood on the floor seemed as much an arrangement as the crimson tulips on the table.

The weapon, a carving knife from a rack near the sink lay near the body. He thought he heard a footfall, but it was phantom. Then he heard a real one. Returning, Sergeant Avery was careful where he stepped. The killer had tracked blood.

"They're coming. You all right, Chief?"

"Go question the neighbors, Eugene. I'll wait here."

Standing alone, he let his mind glide to other things, to the day the old chief pinned a badge on him and gave him a gun, to the evening he and his mother spoke in hushed tones at his father's casket. Neither would have been surprised had his father, whose opinions had always come first, risen to interrupt them. Deeper in the murk of his thoughts was a school desk with a pair of initials dug into the varnish.

He heard abrupt sounds in the house, as if a cover had been lifted and voices let out. An overlarge trooper in full regalia and a detective in mufti appeared and spoke to him. The detective asked a number of quick questions to which he gave automatic answers. Then they sidestepped him and ignored him.

"She put up a fight," the detective said, crouching. "Defensive wounds on her hands."

The trooper said, "Wonder whose broken glasses those are, hers or—"

"Hers," Morgan said.

Rising, the detective pointed here and there. "Those look like sneaker prints." He wore his responsibilities the way judges wear their robes. His gaze shifted. "Haven't touched anything, have you, Chief?"

Morgan went outside, controlled his breathing, and wandered into the garden. A dragonfly—a wire with wings—hovered over a blue grape hyacinth. Slithering from a crowd of daffodils was a garter snake whose head suggested a small inquisitive mind. Its tongue flicked out like a struck match. Though afraid of snakes, Morgan stood his ground.

"Chief!"

Sergeant Avery was running toward him. A cardinal shot out of the magnolia tree, which seemed to stretch its limbs. Sergeant Avery was winded.

"Two houses away. Mrs. Crabtree."

Morgan waited.

"She remembers seeing a kid sneaking through backyards. She thinks she knows who it was."

Morgan, looking up at the sky, said, "Why? Why?"

The detective, whose name was Cleveland, sat with leg over leg in a wing chair in Harry Sawhill's house. Bobby Sawhill sat in a mahogany rocker and rocked. A stiff figure, Chief Morgan remained standing. Harry Sawhill, also on his feet, looked at his son and said, "Just tell the truth, Bobby. You've got nothing to hide."

"I wasn't there," Bobby said, rocking nonchalantly.

"Bobby, sit still."

"But you were in the neighborhood," Cleveland said.

Bobby shook his head, as if coming out of a half sleep. His blue eyes were lusterless. "I was at the library most of the time."

"Did you take out a book?"

"I was reading magazines."

Cleveland smiled like an uncle. His features were bland, as if his face were an afterthought. He was buying time, waiting for a search warrant to be processed. His head turned. "What did you say, Chief?"

Morgan had spoken in words too closely stitched together to be understood. He was staring at Bobby. He spoke again, spacing the words. "Did you know Mrs. Bullard?"

"Who?"

"Did you break into the house back in January when no one was living there?"

"Why would I do that?"

"Maybe you were tired," Morgan said. "Maybe you wanted to lie on her bed."

Something shifted inside Harry Sawhill and deepened the gray look of his face. "What's he talking about, Bobby?"

"Let's take one thing at a time," Cleveland said in a deadly calm voice. "All right, Chief?"

Morgan's gaze did not leave Bobby. For a stunning moment he had a notion of taking him by the throat. He thought of hunters who throw the guts of their kill to their hounds. He said, "You have stains on your sneakers. Did you change your clothes but not your sneakers?"

Cleveland raised a warning hand. "He's going to tell us all about it—aren't you, Bobby?"

"I think I'd better call my brother," Harry Sawhill said.

"A lawyer would be better," said Morgan.

Ben Sawhill arrived out of the dark of the night at the same time the overlarge trooper appeared with the search warrant, another trooper behind him. They dominated the room. "Do you think he did it?" Ben asked the chief in a whisper and received no answer. He glanced at his brother, who looked crushed, and went to his nephew.

"Don't say anything more, Bobby."

Bobby gave out an enigmatic smile. Cleveland had been interrogating him, each question, slowly asked, trailing tentacles. Bobby had said little.

"Stay here," Cleveland said to Morgan and signaled the second trooper to stay put. Harry Sawhill, with an air of inevitability preceding each step he took, led Cleveland and the big trooper out of the room.

Ben placed a caring hand on his nephew's shoulder. "They're going up to your room, Bobby. Stay calm."

The rocker moved gently. Nothing seemed to be touching Bobby, not even his uncle's hand. He was oblivious of Morgan's eyes, which had never left him. Then, as if by accident, their eyes met. Morgan took a step toward him.

"Tell me why."

"Leave him alone," Ben said evenly. "His lawyer's coming."

The lawyer arrived within moments. Morgan knew of him. His name was Ogden, his office in Andover, near Rembrandt's. He was short and stout, with hair fuzzy blond and eyes points of blue. He conferred with Ben in whispers and then glanced at Morgan.

"You shouldn't be here, Chief. This is too personal for you."

"You're absolutely right," Morgan said without moving. He was no longer looking at Bobby but gazing through him, beyond him, as if he could see into another world. His wife was there, and Claudia MacLeod in her best dress was just arriving.

Ben said, "At least sit down."

The others were coming down the stairs. The big trooper carried a plastic bag bearing tainted jeans and a sweatshirt. Harry Sawhill looked as if he wanted to cry. Cleveland nodded to Ogden and said, "I'm going to read him his rights."

"Sure," Ogden said, "but remember he's just a kid."

In a dream, James Morgan was a child again, but his mother was too old to care. His scraped knee went unnoticed, his crying ignored. Waking, he shivered through a vision of himself growing old, aging into uncertainties, losing control of his bladder, chained by memories he didn't want.

By dawn he was showered and shaved and wearing shirt and tie and a dark suit not quite the fit it had once been. Viewing himself in a mirror, he was aware he hadn't made as much of himself as his father had hoped. Once that had mattered to him. Now it didn't.

The telephone rang, jarring him. It was Meg O'Brien. She said, "I knew you'd be up."

"I have to be," he said. "They're going to bury her today."

"Don't come in. There's no need."

"You're in charge, Meg. You always have been."

"No," she said, "but it's nice of you to say so."

He drove from his house to Pleasant Street and on up to Drinkwater's Funeral Home with no intention of going in. He hated the way embalmed faces of the dead hold no meaning. He parked at the curb and sat for several minutes with his eyes closed, his means of saying good-bye before the others. At the Blue Bonnet he sat at the window table where, apparently out of respect, no one joined him. Then Reverend Stottle did. The menu, which never changed, was chalked on a blackboard screwed to the knotty-pine wall. Reverend Stottle ordered scrambled eggs. Morgan had a cup of coffee before him. He looked at his watch.

"Plenty of time," the reverend said. "She's in no rush, nor should we be."

A couple of town hall workers nodded to Morgan on their way out, and Orville Farnham, a selectman, did the same on his way in. Morgan said, "It's the separation that hurts the most."

"But the dead don't stay dead," Reverend Stottle said. "They wander into our dreams."

"Do you believe in heaven?"

"I believe in dreams."

"What about the soul?"

"The soul is fashioned from sounds too distant to be heard. It's wound in light but free of time and has an echo we don't hear."

The scrambled eggs arrived, and Reverend Stottle dug in, his appetite seldom affected by events. Morgan said, "Another question for you. What makes a kid a murderer? Is it a loose wire, a kink in the machinery, a chemical imbalance? Is it a matter of insanity or of cold rationality? Are we talking genetics, upbringing, or something else? Is it pure evil?"

"It's not an easy question, but I will say that if God were Detroit he'd have to recall many of us. Human defects, physical and mental, are rampant."

The waitress returned to the table. "Can't I get you something, Chief?"

"An aspirin."

An hour later he slipped into the Congregational Church, which had filled to standing room only, and poised himself behind a spuming wave of white-haired women. Reverend Stottle conducted the service, and the assistant principal at the regional high school delivered the eulogy, which assigned goodness and generosity to the memory of Claudia MacLeod. Then the church slowly emptied. All the waiting cars bore little funeral flags, except the chief's.

Sergeant Avery stood on Burnham Road and directed the cortege into the timeless green of the cemetery. Much time was needed for the crowd to assemble at the gravesite. Morgan hanging back, seemed more an onlooker than a griever. He edged forward when the ritual was ending and approached Mrs. Perrault and her two sisters. They stood in fixed positions like people in a painting. Mrs. Perrault didn't speak, but her elder sister did.

"We blame you, Chief. You should've stopped her from buying that house."

He stared at Mrs. Perrault, who seemed to have no thoughts, as if her skull were an egg sucked dry.

The other sister said, "Not now, Ida. It isn't the time."

Morgan carried the blame back to the station, where he felt it belonged. Reading sympathy in Meg O'Brien's eyes he looked pointedly away and glimpsed someone in his office, the head of a man half buried in a newspaper held high. "It's that state police detective," Meg said in a near whisper. "I told him you probably wouldn't be back, but he waited anyway."

Cleveland lowered the paper as Morgan stepped past him, and he cast it aside when Morgan settled in behind the desk. They regarded each other through grainy light. "This is a courtesy call, Chief. To bring you up to date."

"Good of you," Morgan said.

"I know she was a friend of yours."

"More than a friend."

"I know that too." Cleveland draped an arm over the back of his metal chair. "We matched the kid's sneakers to the prints at the scene, we even got his fingerprints there, and we got a blood match off his jeans. We got everything, Chief, except a confession. I've never seen a kid so cool. Kinda scary. He admits to nothing."

"He's responsible for two deaths."

"Even if what you say is true, I don't think we can prove it. We got him on this one for sure."

Morgan tightened. "I want to know the motive. I want to know why he did one and then the other. I want to know if the house had any significance. I need answers, Cleveland. I need reasons."

"The kid's in a cloud. We may never know."

"But I have to," Morgan said.

* * *

Harry Sawhill and Trish Becker were alone together at a rear room at his brother's house. It was a room of heavy drapes, wainscoted walls, and club chairs. Harry was at the liquor cabinet, though Trish had told him to stay away from it. His brother had no vodka, only bourbon. He took a belt of it and then another for good measure. Turning, he said, "I don't know my own son. He's a stranger."

Immobile in a club chair, Trish said nothing. Since the murder, the macabre overshadowed the ordinary.

"I don't know anything, Trish, not even myself." He moved toward her and looked down at her. "Are we still going to get married?"

"One thing at a time," she said in a voice that barely carried.

"Stick by me, please. Don't leave me."

Since his son's arrest, she had scarcely left his side, her shock as great as his. His sprang from the horror of it all, hers from an unanswerable question, to which she now gave voice. "If he was going to kill anyone, Harry, why didn't he kill me?"

"Don't say that. We don't know he did."

"Yes, we do."

Ben Sawhill entered the room quietly and dropped into a heavy chair beyond Trish's. Fatigue had cut into his face, but his voice was clear. "It doesn't look good," he said. "They have enough evidence to charge him."

58

Harry teetered. "They're not going to let him go?"

"Didn't you hear me? They're charging him with murder."

"What are you doing for him?"

"Everything I can, Harry." Ben glanced fleetingly at Trish, who seemed inattentive. His voice lifted. "For the time being he's in a holding cell at the state police barracks in Andover. The odd thing is he seems to be enjoying it."

"That's not my Bobby," Harry said forcefully.

"My question is do we know who Bobby is? He's scheduled for psychological evaluation."

"I know my son. He's not a killer." Harry returned to the liquor cabinet. "What's the most we can hope for, Ben?"

"That he won't be tried as an adult."

His first morning at the new place, a whole new world to him, he submitted to a physical examination. He didn't mind the doctor peering into his eyes and ears and down his throat, but he disliked the rest. A nurse who seemed to have more authority than the doctor gave him orders. Standing on a rubber mat, he felt pink and foolish with his clothes off. Staring at him, the nurse's eyes turned beady.

"You sure you're only thirteen?" she asked.

"I'll be fourteen soon."

He lifted his arms while the doctor palpated him and relayed his observations to the nurse, who transcribed them on a yellow sheet of paper fastened to a clipboard. When he stepped on the scale, the nurse adjusted the weights. He looked for a tender light in her eyes but found none.

"Get dressed," she said.

A man in hospital whites took him away.

In the afternoon they wanted to measure the electrical activity of his brain, but he turned stubborn and wouldn't let them. A different doctor wanted to discuss his dreams, but he wouldn't do that either. The room was bare except for a table and the chairs he and the doctor occupied. The chalk-blue walls held no pictures on which he could rest his eyes.

"Is this a prison or a hospital?"

The doctor smiled out of an unblemished complexion. "Neither, Bobby. It's a facility."

"I've been read my rights."

"They don't apply here. Here there's nothing to worry about. What's your earliest memory?"

He could remember far back in his life. He could remember his thumb in his mouth. He could remember being lifted off the potty. What he couldn't remember was the warmth of the womb, but curled up in bed at night, snuggled into the covers, he could reenact his beginnings.

"Come on, Bobby. Give me an answer."

"I don't have one."

"Tell me about your mother."

When the doctor lowered his head, Bobby saw thin places in his hair. "She's dead."

"I know, but tell me about her anyway. Do you miss her?"

He missed coloring books, bedtime stories, toys in his bath. He missed playing store with his mother. Money was Necco candy wafers, which they later ate, thumbprints and all. He missed his mother's smell, her lap. Most of all, he missed knowing she was there.

"Sometimes," he said.

"Some people say that when you lose your mother you lose the world. Do you believe that?"

"I don't know."

"What bothers you the most, Bobby?"

"About what?"

"Anything. Everything."

He didn't like flowers. Red roses were funerals, cemeteries, and white ones were clumps of nothing, the scent of each jumbling living with dying, one no better than the other.

"Nothing," he said.

The doctor tried to bully him with a look. "Are you sure? Do you hate anyone? Yourself, perhaps?"

"No."

"Do you like girls?"

"My cousins are girls."

"You like them?"

"They're OK."

"Do you like women?"

"I guess so."

The doctor went silent. He consulted his notes and then returned his gaze to Bobby. A moment passed as each seemed to reappraise the other. Dropping back in his chair, the doctor said, "I think I know exactly what you're doing, Bobby."

"What am I doing?" He was interested. He wanted to know.

"You're playing an intellectual game with me. You think you're pretty clever. The fact of the matter is you're in trouble. Deep trouble. Aren't you a little scared?"

"What have I got to be scared about?"

"They got the goods on you. That's my understanding."

He said nothing. He felt he didn't have to. His thoughts and the doctor's would meet and mesh in the air. The doctor's stare pressed upon him.

"Some crimes leave no margin for mercy. Yours could be one of them."

Curiosity livened his face. "Am I going to do hard time?"

"I certainly hope so." The doctor gathered his notes, rose from the chair, and stood tall. "But I doubt it."

Chief Morgan was not a welcome visitor, but after a pause Ben Sawhill let him in and led him into a room off the foyer. Open windows let in mild breezes of the evening. Seating himself under a lamp that cast a weak light, Morgan said, "I need your help."

Ben, torn, shook his head. "I can't give it to you. It shouldn't be this way, but we're on opposite sides. Nothing I can do about it."

"Your nephew has killed twice."

Ben hurled up a hand. He didn't want to hear. "I know what you're getting at, and I don't believe it."

"Perhaps you don't want to believe it."

"Look, Chief, I've known you a long time, I respect you, but don't you know what this has done to my brother, not to mention me and my family?"

Morgan spoke in his quietest voice. "Don't you know what this has done to Claudia MacLeod's mother?"

"What exactly do you want?"

"I don't think Bobby should get away with anything. It would be a terrible mistake."

Ben, who had remained on his feet, moved to a window. Restrained and tense, he said, "Are you after justice or revenge?"

"Either one will do," Morgan said, "but it goes beyond that. I know you have influence. I know you and your lawyer are trying to work up a deal with the D.A."

A telephone was ringing somewhere in the house. Then it stopped. Ben, drawing a hand over his forehead, said, "There's no death penalty in Massachusetts, but is that what you want?"

"No," Morgan said softly. "I've never been able to take another person's life. Even in Nam I couldn't."

"Then, for Christ's sake, what do you want?"

"I want him put away for a long time. Not just till he's twenty-one."

Belle Sawhill appeared suddenly in the doorway. Her face was as restrained and tense as her husband's. "It's Trish Becker, Ben. I think you should talk to her."

Ben left. Belle remained. She was not a native of the town, but Morgan considered her one because

63

she was married to a Sawhill and stood apart from other women living in the Heights, as if she were equally at home in both worlds.

"Don't," she said when he started to rise, and he sank back. Her voice, rich and warm, made him comfortable. The black of her hair, clipped short, brought forth the white of her face and the appeal of her features.

"I didn't mean to intrude on your evening," he said.

"It's perfectly understandable." She moved into the room with a silent tread and stood in partial shadow. "Miss MacLeod meant a great deal to you, didn't she?"

He nodded.

"I'm so sorry, Chief. When people we love die, it's always a question of who takes the bigger hit—them or us."

It was a question with two answers, both correct, neither of which he cared to think about. He watched her step from the shadow to make more of herself. Her face reached out.

"I'm worried about my girls. About myself. The truth is, Chief, I'm scared to death."

"Me too," Morgan said.

He'd have said more and laid out his anguish if Ben Sawhill had not returned. Ben looked down at him and said, "I think you'd better leave."

Returning from Harry Sawhill's house, Trish Becker was glad to be home, though she felt no peace of mind. She turned on music, which became too loud. She ran a bath, bubbled it, and soaked for a long time. After draping herself in a heavy towel, she stepped on a scale and quarreled with her body. Clothing herself, sucking in to get the zipper up, she faulted the breadth of her hips for the fit of her jeans.

She had tea and toast for supper and watched television until it hurt her head. Still hungry, she made a sandwich and picked up the phone. She punched out a wrong number before she got the right one. Belle came on the line, and then, after a wait, Ben did.

"Please," she said, "come over here. I need to talk."

She ate a bit of the sandwich and threw the rest away, good liverwurst and tasty cheese. Then she gave herself second and third looks in the mirror before Ben arrived. She was at the door when he rang.

Facing each other in a well-lit room, she told him in heavy tones what was wrong, and he said sharply, "Harry's not your responsibility. Never was."

"I promised to marry him."

"Makes no difference."

"How can I back out at a time like this? He'll fall apart."

"His problem, not yours."

She grappled for a hold on herself, on him. "Don't you want to sit down, Ben?"

"No." He towered. He was strength, the handsome prince in her childhood fantasies, a chunk of her father in him. He said, "You can do anything you want. You're under no obligations."

She fought to steady her voice. "I never liked Bobby. He must've known it."

"What's happened has nothing to do with you."

"I don't know what murder is, Ben. It's for the newspapers, not real life. Can I tell you about a dream I had?"

"No."

She told him anyway. In the dream Harry was the attacker and she the victim. Blood ran in sparkles, as if rubies had been crushed and scattered. "Honest to God, that's the way it looked."

"I think you should get away," he said. "Take another one of your vacations."

Desperate, she swayed close to him. "Everything's wrong. I'm on and off my diet. I'm getting fat, Ben. My breasts are too big. They could knock people over."

"Don't exaggerate yourself."

She jostled against him, her breath a spill. "Hold me for a minute. That's not asking a lot is it?"

Reluctantly he looped an arm around her, and at once she pressed in on him and imparted anxieties and needs through the net of her jersey top and the small rips in her jeans. Seconds later his other arm stretched around her and tightened. Gently he kissed her cheek and ran a hand into her hair. She murmured his name. When he suddenly disengaged and stepped aside, she felt a blissful moment unwind into a sad one, which didn't dull an edge of triumph in her voice.

"Something was almost going to happen, wasn't it, Ben?"

Stepping to the doorway, he concurred with a nod. "But it didn't."

In June Trish Becker and her friend Gloria Eisner left on a European vacation, the beginning weeks nearly ruined by rain, discourteous waiters, and bands of disrespectful young people flaunting their arrogance and bad manners. In Paris Trish stained her most expensive dress, and in Rome she got the runs. Spain was better, the weather gorgeous. Lying on a nude beach she and Gloria appraised other women and ranked the men according to their potential. Later, at a seaside restaurant, Trish grew weepy over wine and wondered what life was all about.

Gloria, pouring more wine, said, "Nothing's perfect, nothing's certain, nothing's permanent, nothing's absolute. If you keep that in mind, you have a chance in life."

"You were always brainier than me."

"I've been through more," Gloria said.

"You have a better body."

"You're eating too much."

"Nerves."

Two days later, though it wasn't on their schedule, they flew to London and checked into Dukes Hotel in Mayfair. In the cozy sitting lounge, where the Duke of Wellington's portrait hung over the fireplace, they sipped strong tea and flirted with a balding Pakistani businessman, who didn't quite know what to make of them. With a grin, he said, "Oh you Americans."

"We're women of the world," Gloria corrected him. "In disguise."

In the week that followed they visited the British Museum, Westminster Abbey, Shepherd Market, and Madame Tussaud's, and saw two plays in the West End. They lunched in pubs on Fleet Street and dined at the Cavendish. They shopped on Regent Street, joined the crowds on Oxford, and strolled through Soho. Relaxing on a bench in St. James's Park, Gloria said, "In New York you look at the beautifully dressed women. In London it's the wonderfully tailored men. I love their breast-pocket hankies, don't you?"

Trish's smile was cryptic. "I don't know what I love. I'd like it to be myself."

In their hotel room, while Gloria was taking a shower, Trish telephoned Harry Sawhill, whose voice was scratchy. Alcohol gave him a dreamless sleep that extended deep into each day. Waking, he told her, he felt he'd passed through death. "When are you coming home?" he asked.

She fudged. She mentioned the possibility of Ireland, the charm of Dublin, Bewley's on Grafton Street. "Have you been there, Harry?"

"Ben told me I shouldn't depend on you, but I do."

She didn't want to hear that. And she didn't want to ask about Bobby. "We've each got to stand on our own two feet. It's the only way."

"You must be having a good time."

"I'm off my diet. I'm inflating myself."

"Bobby's compos mentis."

"What?"

"They say he's in his right mind."

She didn't want to hear anymore. She wanted to swim in quiet waters, and he was dragging her straight back into rough ones. "Help me," she said, her hand clamped over the mouthpiece.

"Come home, Trish. I need you."

Her hand lifted. "Soon, Harry. I'll let you know."

She killed one light and dimmed another. Satin lounging pajamas, varicolored, gave her the appearance of a brilliant bird, predatory but wounded. She crawled into one of the twin beds and drew the covers to her chin. Gloria emerged from the bathroom in a short white robe and peered down at her.

"What's wrong, Trish?"

"He's tearing me up."

"Of course. He knows just where to claw. You never should've called him."

"I don't know what I should do."

Gloria sat on the bed's edge and rubbed the top of a knee still humid from her shower. "Do nothing. Sometimes that's best."

Trish's voice was weak, clinging. "I don't want to be a coward."

"You're living in a man's world, kid. Your only obligation is to stay healthy, positive, and relevant. The rest is birdseed."

"I wish I had your attitude." Her head moving on the pillow, Trish freed a beckoning hand. "Remember when we used to sleep over at each other's house?"

Gloria joined her under the covers and took a share of the pillow. "I remember it well."

"We pretended about boys."

"We pretended a lot of things." Gloria placed an arm over her. "You're shivering."

"It was all make-believe and fun. And innocent."

"Sort of. Though you're right, it was fantasy. Some things about the human mind will never be understood. Intuition is one, and clearly imagination is another." Gloria held her close. "Go to sleep."

"I don't think I can."

Gloria's hand meandered over satin and crept into the privacy of warm skin. "Do you want me to make you come?"

"Yes," she said.

Sherwood, considered state of the art, was a youth detention center situated well west of Boston. Bobby Sawhill entered it in July, which distressed Chief Morgan. "My fault," Morgan said, dropping wearily into a chair near Meg O'Brien's desk. "A double murder charge, he'd have been tried as an adult, no question about it. Now he'll walk when he turns twenty-one."

"Foolish to blame yourself," Meg said.

He knew no one else to blame. He'd been suspicious about Mrs. Bullard's death but had never followed up. A better policeman would have, he told himself.

"You don't know for sure," Meg said, half reading his mind, and answered a radio call from Sergeant Avery, who was taking an hour off to drive his sister to the eye doctor in Andover. She spoke impatiently. "That's terrific, Eugene." And clicked off.

Morgan said, "Yes, I do. In my gut. What I don't know is why. Why Eve Bullard? Why Claudia?" His voice was thin, clinical, without skin. "I've never got over the loss of my wife, but I've gone on. Claudia's death is different. I feel responsible."

A table fan did little to lessen the heat of the day. Meg rose from her desk and tugged at her dress. Burst capillaries on her bare legs resembled ornate stitchery, which endeared her to him. She had been with the department longer than he. Her job, a place to go to each day, was her life. The same was true for him.

"I don't know if I can take the hit," he said.

She angled past Sergeant Avery's desk and opened a portable refrigerator partially hidden by a file cabinet. She returned with two cans of root beer and gave him one, which he gripped firmly but didn't open. She took it from his hand and opened it for him.

"Don't drive yourself crazy," she said.

He smiled. "You know what I also know, like it's written on a blackboard?"

She knew and didn't want to be told. "You could be wrong."

"No, Meg. Sure as I'm sitting here, he'll kill again."

Late in August Harry Sawhill and his brother Ben played an hour of golf at the Bensington Country Club. An hour was the most Harry could manage. The sun got to him, and the clubhouse beckoned. In the lounge, after a moment's hesitation, he ordered tomato juice for himself and beer for Ben. They talked baseball. "Nineteen fifty-one," Ben said, "was a watershed. It was Joe DiMaggio's last year as a Yankee and Mickey Mantle's first."

"I never understood your liking the Yankees over the Red Sox," Harry said. "It wasn't natural, growing up here."

"It was the pinstripes," Ben said. "It fit the image I wanted of myself. Now, however, I favor the Sox."

"That's a switch."

"We show more compassion as we grow older."

Ben's beer was in a tankard, the head running over. Harry added celery salt to his tomato juice and ventured a sip. Getting away from baseball, Ben turned to what was really on his mind.

"You doing the wise thing, Harry?"

"I want to be happy. Nothing wrong with that, is there?"

"Nothing in the world. I want you to be happy."

"But you think I'm doing wrong. Go ahead, say it."

"No, I think it's wonderful. If it's what you both want."

"Why wouldn't it be? Nobody wants to be alone." Reaching into a silver dish, Harry came up with a nervous fistful of cashews. "There's one thing."

"Yes, there's that, isn't there?"

"I don't know how to tell Bobby."

On a Saturday afternoon in September Harry Sawhill and Trish Becker were married in Reverend Stottle's living room. Ben Sawhill and Gloria Eisner were witnesses. Her blond hair tied back, Trish wore a powder-blue suit with a diamond brooch. Marrying for the second time, she felt repossessed, like an automobile. Harry, standing gray and rigid, was not sure it was real and for a single second confused Trish with his first wife. Someone prodded him, and he kissed the bride.

Then Ben did.

CHAPTER FOUR

Mr. Grissom, the administrator of Sherwood, considered himself enlightened, progressive, and benevolent. A light-skinned African-American, he considered himself free of racial resentments and clever enough to play by his own rules. He said, "I'm not putting you in a dormitory, Sawhill. They'd make meat of you, you know what I mean?"

Bobby stood before Mr. Grissom's desk. "I think so."

Mr. Grissom's mobile face gained speed as he spoke. "You'll share a room with an older boy. Dibble. He's seventeen, smartest student here. That's what we call you boys here. You listen to Dibble, you'll do all right. By the way, he's black. That bother you?"

"I've never known anybody black."

"That's your misfortune."

"I'm white."

"I can see that. Here, that doesn't count."

"What are you, sir? Are you black or white?"

"I'm neither. That means I'm in the middle, and that makes me fair and square."

Mr. Grissom stood up from his desk. Bobby had thought Mr. Grissom was tall but now saw he was short and wiry and, like everyone else, wore the uniform of Sherwood. Gray sweats.

"You play with yourself, Sawhill?"

Bobby blushed. "Sometimes."

"Keep it to a minimum. Masturbation isn't punishable, but homosexuality is. Drugs are taboo. So's lying, stealing, and acting up, especially in the classroom. Good grades count here, give you extra privileges. Dibble will clue you in on the rest. Any questions?"

"What's he in for, sir?"

"Same as you. Welcome to Sherwood."

The whitewashed room was impeccably neat, furnished with two army cots, two wall lockers, and a writing table, nothing on the walls except a shelf lined with paperbacks. The occupant stood loose and tall in a T-shirt and low-waisted jeans. He was a runner, his skin ivory black, his body honed for speed and supple strength. "That's mine," he said, pointing to one cot and then the other. "That's yours. What's your name?"

"Bobby."

"Baby name. I'm Dibble. You're on probation. Six weeks from now, it works out, you can call me Dibs. Nice watch you're wearing."

"It's a Seiko."

"Rich kid, huh? You get things from home, you

share everything. Choice of two things, one better than the other, I get it."

Bobby nodded. He liked Dibble's voice, swift and clear, as much a man's as a boy's, and he liked the italicized stubble on Dibble's jaw.

Dibble said, "The table's mine. You don't touch anything on it. Another thing you don't do is cry. Bad things happen, you live with 'em. Only one thing scares Grissom, that's a kid killing himself. It puts him and Sherwood in jeopardy."

"I wouldn't do that."

"You never know."

Bobby liked Dibble's stance, relaxed and easy, real cool, thumbs hooked into the top of his jeans. He wished he had Dibble's body but knew his bones were different. He said, "How come you get to wear jeans?"

"It's a privilege. I'm the only one who's got it. You got no privileges at all. First six weeks you do toilet duty."

"Am I going to get raped?"

"Not by me." Dibble looked him over. "You're big, but you're soft. Work out in the gym all you can."

Bobby smiled. "You don't talk black."

"That so? You talk sissy. You got a way to go, kid. Can you take pain?"

"I don't know."

Dibble slapped him hard across the face. His head shot back. His whole face down into his neck felt the shock. His eyes watered, but he didn't cry.

"Good boy," Dibble said.

* * *

A bank of urinals led to a series of stalls, opposite which was a row of sinks. Beyond was a shower room. Mops and brushes, yellow soap and water, ammonia and deodorizers kept the place clean and smelling right. In charge was a white boy called Duck because he waddled like one. Bobby was his assistant, but Duck did the most work because he took pride in it.

Bobby said, "What are you in for?"

"I touched girls," Duck said quickly, as if he'd also taken pride in that. He was older than Bobby but smaller and had a happy face.

"How long you been here?"

"I don't keep track." He ran the head of a mop through a wringer and squeezed it dry. When he scrubbed the urinals, his energy was manic.

Dibble, wearing a nylon athletic jacket over his T-shirt, came in a little later to inspect the place, which he did quickly, a few glances here and there, while Bobby and Duck stood at attention. "Good job," he said and patted Duck on the shoulder. "Did you tell Sawhill you're silly in the head?"

Duck grinned. "He knows."

"And what am I?"

"You're coal waiting to become diamond."

"Good boy, you got it right. And what did I tell you Sawhill is?"

Duck's grin turned sheepish. "Bobby's a turd waiting to be flushed."

"Does he know you're in charge? Does he do what you tell him?"

"I do," Bobby said.

78

When Dibble left, Duck said, "He's the best."

Away from the toilets Duck stuck close to Bobby. In the classroom, repeating grades, Duck did poorly while Bobby, seated beside him, often let him copy from his paper, which the teacher didn't seem to mind. Neither was much good in the gym. They had no grace in tossing up a basketball, no eye for the basket, no feel for the ball, though no one openly made fun of them. They were Dibble's charges.

In the recreation room Dibble put on shows. No one, not even when he spotted points, could beat him at table tennis. His arm was a steel whip, his serves invisible. When he used English, the ball went crazy. Watching, squeezing Bobby's arm, Duck said, "I love him."

Bobby said, "Me too."

Bobby liked it best when he and Dibble were alone together in their room, even when he couldn't make a sound because Dibble was reading or thinking or simply relaxing. In the silence he imagined a sharing of secrets so sensitive they didn't have words. His eyes relished Dibble in repose.

On his feet, Dibble said, "Grissom's scheduled you for counseling. Therapy. They're gonna want to know what makes you tick. What makes you laugh. What makes you sweat. My advice, Sawhill, is don't let anybody get in your head."

"I never have."

Dibble smiled. "You're not as dumb as I thought."

* * *

Married, she kept her name. She was still Trish Becker. Harry Sawhill kept his house, and she put hers on the market without moving out. They lived in both places, back and forth, a couple of weeks in his house, longer in hers. Hers didn't sell because she kept the price inordinately high, and as abruptly as she had put it on the market she took it off.

Harry, ensconced in her bed, called to her. "I thought you hated this house. I know I do. It's far too big."

"I'm not letting it go for a song." She was stepping onto a scale in the bathroom. She weighed in at a hard hundred-thirty pounds, which was her essential shape.

"What's the real reason?"

"I want my children to know they have their home to come to."

"What's the matter with my house?"

"That's Bobby's house. This is theirs."

He was silent for a moment. "You hate him."

She was brushing her teeth. After spitting out, she said, "I fear him. Don't you?"

"He's my son."

"He's not mine."

When she entered the bedroom, Harry drew aside the covers on her side of the bed. "We really married, Trish, or we just pretending?"

Her thin gown clung to the expanse of her hips. Through the translucency her groin divulged the true color of her hair, which was not blond. She extinguished the bedside lamp and darkened the room. "Ask Reverend Stottle. He said the words."

Settling into bed, she took comfort in the knowledge she would not be alone through the night. Should a bad dream wake her, she could reach out for warmth, provided Harry wasn't in the throes of a cold sweat. He rolled against her with no alcohol on his breath. He hadn't touched a drop in a week.

"Shall we?"

"If you want," she said.

When he rested a hand on her abdomen, she remembered her panic when her first marriage was disintegrating and her need for refuge consuming. When he kissed her on the mouth, heavily, greedily, she remembered lying lumpish for men she didn't want, men who considered her windfall.

"Where are you going, Harry?"

He was dipping under the covers, raising them, loosing them. He was down on her, licking a stamp. Where would he mail her? Was she first class or bulk?

It wasn't working.

She forced him back up. Eschewing the inferior position, she straddled him, bore down, and took command. Her fantasies flew to his brother and then to her first husband. She connived with both, two phantoms carrying her down the stretch. A moment later she collapsed as Harry's head jerked up.

"What are you laughing for?"

"I always do," she said, controlling herself.

"Not that loud."

"I'm happy."

He spoke with sadness. "No, you're not."

She spoke with practicality. "Next best thing."

Chief Morgan finished buying take-out at the deli counter in Tuck's when a slight figure appeared at his elbow without warning. A voice said, "Do you miss her, James? Do you miss her as much as I do?"

He turned slowly, a weight on his shoulders. "I miss her in my own way, Mrs. Perrault."

"But you can find another woman. I won't ever have another daughter." Mrs. Perrault's eyes were teardrops. Her hair was tightly permed, but the hues were gone. Wrinkles in her face reached out. "Why wasn't that boy put away for life?"

He answered quietly, his tone deliberate. "His uncle got him a good lawyer."

"Sawhills have money. That's the long and short of it. They have money, and I have no daughter. What am I to do with the little that's left of my life?"

He had no answer, only a rush of memories. He remembered the tint of Claudia's skin, the small mole between her breasts, the childhood collection of abscess scars in her underarms.

A critical moment passed.

"Do you eat your supper alone, James?"

"Usually," he said, "but sometimes I have it at the Blue Bonnet."

"Would you like to eat with us? My sisters aren't the best company, but you're welcome."

"Maybe sometime," he said.

They stepped aside for other customers, Morgan clutching his take-out bag, not all that much in it for a grown man. Mrs. Perrault said, "You probably think I do, but I don't blame you. Claudia had a mind of her own, but we didn't often let her use it. We wanted her to ourselves. My sisters don't see it, but we were selfish."

"She was just looking for a life of her own," he said. "That's the whole of it."

They stepped out of the store. Mrs. Perrault had in her arms a small bag of groceries. He wanted to carry it for her, but she shook her head. "I'm able."

Claudia's Dodge Colt was parked behind the store. The sight of it hurt his eyes. "I didn't know you drove," he said.

"I do a lot for myself now."

He opened the driver's door, stepped back, and gazed up at a sky of restless white clouds jostled by whatever disturbances roamed that high. Mrs. Perrault settled in behind the wheel, fastened her seat belt, and looked out at him.

"We have to sell that awful house. I don't think of it as Claudia's but as Mrs. Bullard's. I can't imagine who would want to buy it."

Nor could he. Were he felonious, reckless, not the police chief, he would burn it down. Were he an expanded version of himself, he would take all matters into his own hands. He closed the driver's door and started to walk away. He stopped and turned around when Mrs. Perrault called to him, her small face framed in the open window.

"I wish you were the Almighty," she said.

He looked at her wonderingly. Yet he knew what she was going to say.

"So you could bring her back, James."

On a Sunday afternoon Ben Sawhill and his brother strolled the back reaches of his property. Towering pines dropped golden needles, several to a pack. A blizzard of birds flew overhead, swerved in a great arc, and vanished into the blue. Ben said, "Bobby's uncooperative. He's refused counseling. Otherwise, Grissom says he's doing all right."

"How can he be doing all right if he's not getting help?"

"One thing at a time, Harry."

"Why doesn't he want me to visit him? I'm his father. You're his uncle. Why doesn't he want to see you?"

"He needs time to adjust. Grissom says you should write him once a week if possible, even if you don't get answers."

"I wouldn't know what to say. On paper it's different, harder. The words become permanent. Damn it, Ben, Bobby and I were never close. His mother's death did something to both of us."

They approached the start of maple and oak splurging colors. Leaves were trailing away, and the woods were opening up, showing empty shelves. Harry shuddered.

"Is my kid a monster?"

"Something's terribly wrong with him, that's certain."

84

"My fault, Ben? Is that what people say?"

"Doesn't matter what people say. We're Sawhills."

"I don't know what I'd do if I didn't have Trish. How's Belle taking it?"

"She's still shaken, of course."

"The twins?"

"Hard to tell," Ben said. "They're still so young."

"Maybe they could write to Bobby."

"Maybe."

They skirted the woods. Once the area had been all woods, the Heights not even a gleam in a developer's eye. In boyhood they had known all the straying paths, the sudden openings, the secret nooks, and could enter rooms of antique fern and emerald moss, with pets in the corners, a fleeing snake here, a chipmunk there. They were Boy Scouts. Ben knew birds. The gold of a finch was money in the bush. The tanager adored his mate. Harry knew droppings. He knew a skunk's scat from a possum's, and he knew the leavings of a fox and the pellets of an owl.

"It's getting chilly," Harry said with a shiver.

Ben, gazing at the sun, didn't feel the chill. He saw the sun as gold, the money that keeps the earth alive. "Zip up your jacket."

Harry noted the shadows in the woods and saw danger. Milkweed let loose parachutes. Sumac blazed. He liked autumn but dreaded what would follow. Too much isolating darkness and cold. He hated the holiday season. Too much sadness.

"When we were kids, Ben, I was the boss. Now you are. I take my cues from you."

85

"I don't see it that way."

"You always had more drive, certainly more brains."

Ben sighed. "Let's not get on that subject, OK?"

"I'm quoting the old man's opinion. He said he didn't know how to deal with me."

"You going to drop it or not, Harry?"

"I'm scared, that's what I'm getting to. What will I do with Bobby when he comes out?"

"That's a good while yet. We'll figure it out then."

They began retracing their route back to the house. The sun was in and out, hunching behind this cloud and then that one. Another storm of birds appeared.

"Starlings," Ben said.

Harry zipped up his jacket. "I wouldn't know. You knew birds, I knew shit."

On Bobby Sawhill's last working day in the toilets, Duck said, "I'm gonna miss you. I never had a pal before."

"Me neither." Bobby ran two scrub brushes together under running water to clean them. "We'll still see each other."

"But not as much. Maybe you could ask to stay."

"It's already been decided. They're putting me in the library."

"I'll always be in the toilets," Duck said and made suds with a big yellow bar of soap. Then he smiled. "Smells good in here, don't it, Bobby? I keep it nice."

They were still at the sinks when they heard the

scuffs of someone's heavy sneakers. In the mirrors they saw the rangy snakelike figure of a bad character named Ernest, who was bare-chested in sweatpants, olive-skinned, tattooed on one arm. The tattoo was a skull and bones. He had a shaved head and hooded eyes.

"You're not supposed to use these toilets," Duck said into a mirror, his tone of authority tentative. "You're supposed to use the ones for Dorm C."

Ernest grinned. Dorm C was for youths no longer boys, short-timers headed for a halfway house or state prison. "I go where I want, Duck, always have. I shit, you come wipe me, OK?" His grin widened. "Or Sawhill can do it, if he's got your touch."

Duck changed color. "You're not supposed to talk to us that way."

"That's right." Ernest ambled up behind them and threw his torso close to Bobby's. "You're Dibble's boys. His little whiteys."

Bobby spoke to his own reflection. "I'm not so little."

"But you can't stand up to me, can you? I could slit your throat with my fingernail."

Bobby held his breath, and so did Duck. Laughing, Ernest sauntered off not toward the stalls but to the urinals, which hung from the wall like giant peeled eggs. Poised at one, legs spread, he pissed mostly on the floor. Leaving, he said, "Clean it up, Duck."

After several seconds passed and they were sure he was gone, Duck said, "He's getting meaner. Time's running short."

"He's getting out?"

"He's graduating. Going to the real place. He won't be so tough there."

"Who'd he kill?" Bobby asked.

"His whole family. He was high." Duck carried mop and pail to the urinals and began swabbing. "How many did you kill, Bobby?"

Images working into the forefront of his mind, Bobby held up a finger and then added another, which stirred memories. The memories, like pages in a coloring book, required crayons.

"I've never killed anybody," Duck said. "Don't know if I could."

"It's not hard," Bobby said.

Mr. Grissom summoned Bobby to his office and viewed him with an unsparing eye. "How's Dibble treating you, Sawhill?"

Bobby smiled immediately. "He lets me call him Dibs now."

"That says something. In fact, it says a lot. Anybody giving you trouble?"

"No, sir."

"Know when to be brave, know when to back down. I like heroes, but I like smart cowards better, boys who know how to look after themselves. You like your job in the library?"

"I miss the toilets," Bobby said.

Mr. Grissom let that pass. His active face speeded up. "So far all reports on you have been good, except for one thing. Why are you resisting counseling? I don't understand that. Aren't there things you want to talk about, get off your chest? Don't you want to be a happy person?"

"I am happy."

Mr. Grissom went silent for a few moments, the movement in his face subsiding. "Something else I don't understand. Why don't you want to see your family?"

"You said I didn't have to."

"Doesn't mean I think it's right. Your uncle calls every week to see how you're doing. Your father got on the line once, and I talked with him. Don't they mean anything to you?"

Bobby groped through a murk of feelings, careful not to vanish into an emotional sinkhole. "I don't know," he said.

"I see you got a letter the other day. Who was that from?"

"My cousins. They're twins."

"They mean anything to you?"

"They're just kids," Bobby said and prayed Mr. Grissom would not delve deeper into his family. He didn't want his mother's name mentioned. He didn't want her memory disturbed.

"You can write to them, you know. Nothing stopping you."

"Yes, sir."

"OK, Sawhill, I guess that's about it for now. You keep your nose clean, a few months from now you'll have treats."

Bobby brightened. "Treats, sir?"

"Dibble will tell you about it when it's time. You keep quiet about it for now."

"Yes, sir."

"I like you, Sawhill. Already you're one of my better boys."

CHAPTER FIVE

Seated near a log fire, Ben Sawhill was engrossed in a newspaper, his eye fastened to the financial page. Seated nearby, Belle Sawhill used a magazine as a lapboard on which she was trying to write a letter to her sister in Seattle. The letter was an attempt to clear her mind, but each word was forced. Finally she put pen and paper aside and let the magazine slip between her knees.

"I'm worried, Ben. I'm worried about the girls. I don't want them writing to Bobby anymore."

"What's the harm?" Ben folded his paper in half. "We can't simply cut him out of our lives, pretend he doesn't exist."

"That's exactly what I want to do. He's not your son. He's only your nephew."

Ben stared quietly at the fire, tongues of flame leaping up as if to tell a story. "I'll do whatever you want," he said. "I worry too."

The words subdued her, made her rethink her position without changing it. "Worst is the guilt I

91

feel. After his mother died, when we had him with us, I should have done more for him. Spent more time with him."

"How could you? You had two newborns on your hands."

"I had help. I could've made time, but I had eyes only for my babies. They're so precious to me." She cocked an ear. The twins were in their room, doing their homework. "When they're alone together they become one. They're two heartbeats, a single soul. When they stare at each other, I wonder what they see."

"We've been blessed, Belle. Harry hasn't. He's had nothing but heartache."

"I know. Poor Harry. How's his drinking?"

"On and off. Thank God he has Trish, but I don't know how long she'll put up with him."

"Quite a while, Ben, have no fear."

He gave her exceptional attention. "Why do you say that?"

She rose and stood by the fire, her hands pressed into the baggy pockets of a coat sweater. Firelight streaked her black hair. "She's in love with you, you know that."

"That's not my fault. I've done nothing to encourage her."

"Is she hard to resist?"

"Not in the least."

His words warmed her more than the fire did, though she shuddered, as if she had survived a dangerous moment. "I'm sorry, Ben. I'm being silly, but lately everything's a threat."

"How the hell could I love anyone but you? Impossible."

She withdrew a letter from the right pocket of the sweater, the handwriting on the small envelope immature. "They've given me another one to mail, but I'm not going to do it. Do you mind?"

"I think you're wrong, but I don't mind."

She tossed the letter into the fireplace and watched it burn. The flames looked happy.

Harry Sawhill was drunk. In the dark a chair swung in front of him and banged his knee. Reeling, he felt the edge of a table stab him. Trish, reading in bed, heard a thump. Barefoot, she rushed down the stairs, switched on the kitchen light, and found him sitting on the floor, nursing his wounds, and crying. His eyes swerved up.

"I'm no good, Trish. No damn good."

Without saying anything, she tended to agree. Leaning over him, she gripped him under the arms. "Get up," she said.

He couldn't, or he didn't want to. His weight was too much for her. She let go and staggered back, her body big and busy in thin pajamas.

"Not my fault," he said. "I still don't know my way around your house."

"Wouldn't have happened in your house, huh?" Her voice was spiteful. Then it softened. "You hurt?"

He wiped his nose with the back of his hand. "I hate your house."

She hated it too. It was the fruits of a failed marriage, part of a payoff from a man she'd always known she'd lose. She had loved him too much. Harry was another matter. Dropping to one knee, she swept an arm around him. "Where do you hurt?"

"Everywhere."

She hugged him lightly, as if giving limited love to a child not hers. His nose was running, needed another wipe. Damned if she was going to do it. "Get up, Harry. Don't make mama mad."

He shuffled about, drew up a foot, needed help, more than she could give without more effort from him. "You're everything to me," he said. "You're the cream in my coffee."

"And you're the fly in my ointment. Come on, Harry, give it another try."

He used brute strength she didn't know he had. On his feet he tottered and grabbed the table edge and then her arm for support. She threw her belly against his to steady him. For an instant they looked like dancers.

"You're not going to be sick, are you?"

"No, I swear," he said.

She helped him up the stairs, which involved only a few stumbles. In the bedroom she undressed him and got him under the covers, where he began to shiver. She didn't intend to join him, but he wanted her with him.

"Hold me," he said.

She climbed into bed and did what he wanted, the least she could do, part of the marriage bargain, wifely duties, motherly concerns. They all hit upon her. His breath was in her face.

"Are you going to leave me?"

"No, I'll never leave you," she said and felt him drifting into a stupor. When he began to snore, she said, "And you're right, Harry. You're no good at all."

They played poker in the fire barn, nickel and dime, a quarter limit, a table set up near the pumper. Malcolm Crandall, the town clerk, fluttered the cards and made them crackle and pop. He was a serious player and a fast dealer. He shot cards around the table, two down, one up. "Seven-card stud," he said unnecessarily. It was what he always played. He disliked anything fancy or out of the ordinary. "Your bet, Doc."

"What?"

"You got high card. Bet!"

Old Doctor Skinner was semiretired and had failing vision. He bet a nickel. Everyone stayed in except Chub Tuttle, a volunteer fireman whose real job was roofing and carpentry. Chub played timid, as if he were using grocery money.

Malcolm dealt again, a card to each, face up, and scowled at his, which indicated nothing. He perpetually scowled. He was heavyset and surly, with latching brows and a permanent pucker. Years ago when he was in the army a sucker punch permanently disfigured his nose. "You're high, Chief."

Chief Morgan bet a dime, and Sergeant Avery, an erratic player, raised it a quarter.

"Why the hell did you do that?" Malcolm demanded. "You haven't got anything."

"You don't know what I got."

"You don't play right, Eugene. You throw everything off."

The chief said, "You in or out, Malcolm?"

Malcolm fed the pot and glared. His jealousy of Morgan went back to high school when each had competed for the same girls, Claudia MacLeod among them. Spinning out more cards, he said, "What do you think of Harry Sawhill marrying the bimbo from the Heights?"

Still high man, Morgan bet another dime. Sergeant Avery raised a quarter. Morgan said, "I don't think anything of it."

Doctor Skinner, dropping out, said, "What bimbo?"

"It's Malcolm's way of speaking," Morgan said. "Play cards."

On the last card Sergeant Avery, who had misread his hand, had nothing. Malcolm, who had caught a third deuce, dropped his sudden smile when Morgan, realizing he had a flush, laid it out.

"I had to win sometime."

It was the doctor's deal. Chub Tuttle, whom he had brought into the world, shuffled for him because his fingers were arthritic. "Same game," he said to placate Malcolm. The deal was slow, the bets fast, though none of the up cards showed promise.

Malcolm said, "How come his kid got a break? You have anything to do with that, Chief?"

Morgan knew he was being baited and didn't respond. "Make sure you know what you're doing this time, Eugene."

Sergeant Avery was raising again but with a keener eye on the cards. Bucking foolish odds, he filled an inside straight and beat Malcolm's two pairs.

Malcolm said, "I was wearing your badge, I'd have done things different."

It was Morgan's deal, five-card stud, quarter bets only. Morgan's up card was an ace. Chub Tuttle immediately dropped out. Malcolm snorted.

"Christ, don't you ever stay in?"

He beat Morgan's ace with a pair of eights. Morgan said, "What would you have done different?"

"No sense talking about it." He raked in quarters. "Too late."

Morgan persisted. "I'm curious."

"You wouldn't understand."

Sergeant Avery had the deal, draw poker, guts to open. Chub Tuttle opened with a dime, threw away no cards, and won a small pot with a full house.

"The reason you wouldn't understand," Malcolm said, "is you're not a real cop. You don't even carry a gun."

Two attendants stood at each end of the dining hall, where breakfast was served in two thirty-minute shifts. Breakfast was toast, cornflakes, an overripe banana, and as much tomato juice as anyone wanted. Bobby Sawhill carried his tray to Dibble's table and, looking frantically around, said, "Where's Duck? Duck's not here."

Dibble was in charge of a table of twelve. Duck's chair was vacant. Dibble said, "He's sick."

"Is he going to be all right?"

"I'm not a doctor."

"Where is he?"

"In the infirmary."

Bobby picked at his breakfast, eating only some of the cornflakes. The boy sitting on his left, a Hispanic with the eyes of an owlet, said, "Can I have your toast?"

In the afternoon Bobby received permission to visit the infirmary. Duck's last name was printed on a tag tied to the end of a metal cot. The name was fat and Polish, senseless to the ignorant eye. It didn't look like a name to Bobby, simply a jumble of letters. Bobby's voice quavered.

"I didn't know."

Duck smiled. He had been sick for three days without telling anyone. Food had come up on him. Rocking with pain, his body had convulsed, then crumbled. An attendant had carried him in his arms to the dispensary and later wheeled him into the infirmary.

"What's the matter with you?"

"I got an ulcer. Sometimes it bleeds."

"Bad?"

"No big deal," Duck said, surprised that Bobby seemed worried. He had always been sickly. His childhood was rickets and ringworm.

"You don't look too good."

"I'll be back soon. Who's doing the toilets?"

"Doesn't matter, Duck. It'll always be your job."

" 'Cept when I get out for good. Then they'll

have to get someone else. Whatcha looking sad for, Bobby?"

He didn't want to leave, he wanted to hold Duck's hand, but a female nurse who needed to do something with pills and a needle said, "Sorry, doll, you can't stay."

At suppertime he ate nothing but a sliver of cranberry sauce. Leaning over his plate, he said, "He's not going to die, is he, Dibs?"

"Why would he want to do that?" Dibble said, buttering a thin slice of white bread. "He's got it made here."

"You're not just saying that, are you?"

"Would I do that? Who loves you, Sawhill?"

"You do, Dibs."

The Hispanic boy touched Bobby's elbow. "Can I have your hamburg?"

Harry Sawhill sat in a private section of the visiting room and waited for Bobby. He ran a nervous hand over his head. In the past few months the hair on top had thinned into uncertainty. His face was haggard. Ten minutes later he was staring into the blue of his son's eyes.

"I'm supposed to be in class," Bobby said, hands tucked into the pouch pocket of a sweatshirt.

"Mr. Grissom says it's all right." Harry was on his feet, his voice tense and uneasy. "You look good, Bobby. Leaner and more muscular."

"I work out. Why are you here?"

"To see you. Why else?" Harry tried to force a

smile and failed. He spoke rapidly. "I got married, Bobby. To Mrs. Becker."

There was no response, no reaction. Bobby looked at his watch. "I'm missing algebra."

Harry had a few thoughts about going mad and then eased away from them. Tightening his shoulders, he said, "Do you know how much I loved your mother?"

"I don't remember her."

"Yes, you do. Then she died, I died too for a while. Part of me is still dead. Do you know what I'm telling you?"

Bobby shoved his hands deeper into the pouch. "She lied to me. She said she wouldn't die."

"She couldn't help it."

Bobby's eyes hinted that he had something to say about that but never would. He simply gazed at his father and said, "I'm a killer."

Harry heard the ring of a school bell from a distant part of the building. He heard the traffic of feet in corridors. He remembered a teacher at Pearson Grammar School, Miss Mulvey, who wore frilly blouses over wire-cup bras, which made her breasts fascinating to eighth-grade boys. He said, "Yes, I know."

"Don't you want to ask me anything?"

"Would you tell me?"

Bobby swaggered. "No."

Reaching the point again where he felt he might fall apart, Harry stepped back. His concern for himself began to outweigh his obligation to Bobby.

"I don't want you to come here again," Bobby said.

"Why not?" He felt frustration and anger. "For Christ's sake, why not?"

"This is my home," Bobby said. "Not yours."

Bobby was all smiles. Sitting with Dibble on a bleacher bench in the gym, he said, "You were right. Duck is OK."

"Told you he would be. You don't listen."

They were watching a basketball game, two teams from Dormitory C. The best players were of color, their bodies serpents, their movements nature's gift to the game, in which the two white players looked out of step, stripped of purpose. One of them threw up an air ball.

"He says he prayed. Is there a God, Dibs?"

"Sure, I see him in dreams. He's a black guy like me, but he doesn't see me. I think he's trying to pass."

"Jesus wasn't black."

"Who says?"

A whistle blew. Ernest had fouled somebody. He wasn't the best player, but he was the most aggressive. His shaved head, hooded eyes, and tattooed arm made him menacing. Dibble rolled his eyes.

"He shouldn't be playing. He lost his privileges."

Bobby munched on a candy bar. "What did he do?"

"Don't eat when you talk to me. I don't want you spitting my way. He broke a new kid's jaw for playing his radio too loud."

Bobby crunched up the candy wrapper and lowered his voice. "He bothered Duck again."

"How so?"

"You know."

Ernest threw for three points and missed, but the ball bounced off the rim and was in his hands again. He zigzagged, faked, leaped, and stuffed the ball in. His mates high-fived him, but the ref called him for an offensive foul. Dibble frowned.

"Why didn't he tell me?"

"He's ashamed."

Dibble shrugged. "I can't be everywhere at once."

In their room Dibble read a newspaper. He was a current event, up on everything. Then he looked through books he'd told Bobby to bring him from the library. Three were by Dickens. He had read them before, several times.

Bobby said, "How come you like him so much?"

"He writes about the good and bad, nothing in between. The bad always pretend they're good, but you know they'll be brought to their knees in the end. That's what keeps you reading. You want to see the bastards grovel." Dibble stretched out on his cot and doubled a pillow to prop his head. "Tell me, Sawhill, did you really pop two people?"

Bobby nodded. "I really did."

"Both women, right?"

For the first time since arriving at Sherwood, Bobby felt an invasion of his innermost privacy, a threat to his balance. "Why can't things be done without a reason?"

"There's always a reason." Dibble smiled. "But that doesn't mean you have to know it."

Bobby had an image of Mrs. Bullard, the lady with the roses, but he had no attachment to the memory and let it drift away. The image of the other woman, young, pretty, lingered a second or two longer. "Who did you kill, Dibs?"

"Doesn't matter."

"But you killed someone."

"I didn't pull the trigger," Dibble said. "Somebody else did, but I was there. When I kill, it'll be somebody important."

"Then you don't know how it feels."

"How does it feel, Sawhill?"

"Like you're someplace else."

The two of them still awake, Bobby spoke through the dark. "Would you kill Ernest?"

Dibble drew a sharp breath. "You didn't listen."

"If he touched me, I'd kill him."

"You don't have perspective, Sawhill. Doing Ernest would put your future in the joint, and you wouldn't have one there, take my word for it."

Bobby pulled the covers under his chin. Often he had no ability to express his feelings, to spring words from his heart.

He said simply, "You're good to me, Dibs."

"I got honor. Rest of the guys here don't. And you, Sawhill, you got hang-ups. Grissom says the biggest is about your mother. Is that right?"

"I don't talk about her."

"What's the problem? She's dead, right?"

"She's inside me."

"My mother burned to death. She was soot on a fireman's face. I tell it as it is, Sawhill. You oughta try doing that."

"She was sick inside. Cancer."

"There you go."

Bobby didn't want to go on talking about her and lay quiet. He heard rain rattling on the window and wondered what month it was. He had forgotten. "What else did Mr. Grissom say about me?"

"Said you're emotionally immature. I could've told him that."

"He told me I was one of his best boys. He said I'm going to have a treat and you'll tell me about it when it's time. When's it going to be time?"

"When I think you can handle it. Grissom wants to keep us all straight, so every once in a while we get a treat. Big time."

"What's the treat, Dibs? Can't you tell me?"

"You saying you can't guess? Jesus, Sawhill. It's a woman."

Bobby went silent. He pulled the covers over his face. He was confused, hurt. After several moments he spoke through the blanket. "What about what you and I do?"

"That's kid stuff," Dibble said. "Go to sleep."

A towel wrapped around his loins, Ernest lay on a bench in the shower room. Dozing, he looked like a molting cobra with skin covering its eyes. The eyes opened. "Whatcha looking at, Duck?"

Duck kept his distance. "You're not supposed to be here. It's not your shower room."

"You gonna put me out? Come let me see you do it."

"You wouldn't talk this way, Dibs was here."

"But he ain't here. Just you and me. Heard you were sick, Duck. Even heard you weren't gonna make it."

"God made me better."

"Nice fella, God. He must like you. I like you too." Ernest raised his head and motioned with it. "Come do what I want."

Duck was trembling and tried not to show it. He tried to hold back tears. "What d'you want me for? You gonna have a woman pretty soon."

"Can't wait."

The tears came. "I don't wanna be hurt again."

"What's a little pain between friends?" Ernest stripped off the towel and pitched his voice high, like a girl's. "Come please me."

Duck began backing off slowly, then swiftly.

Ernest leaped up in a pretense of pursuit. "I'll get you later, Duck. Count on it."

Some of the boys from Dormitory B, ages sixteen through eighteen, were already in the visitor's room. The women arrived presently, six of them, chatting and laughing. Two were white, one was Hispanic, and the other three were African American. Dibble appeared. He was in charge and moved among them. He knew them all, and they knew him and liked him. One of the white women ran a hand up his arm.

"You gonna be one of mine, Dibs?"

"Not this time," he said with a false smile of regret. "But you know I love you."

"Sure," she said mockingly. Her name was Virginia, her blond hair fool's gold. She was twenty-six years old, her anus abused, her vagina a gully, her insides awaiting a hysterectomy. "I know who you want. You want Sharon."

He glanced over his shoulder and glimpsed Bobby poised in the doorway, hesitant to enter. "That's the kid rooming with me. Wet behind the ears."

"I'll take him," Virginia said quickly and then slowly frowned over Dibble's lack of expression. "What's the matter? Ain't I good enough?"

"It's his first time, Ginny. You understand."

"Yeah, you're a real prick, Dibble."

Sharon was the other white woman, her breasts raised and pinched together under a tight top cut low. She had a moody voice and showgirl legs. "I'll take five, Dibs, counting you, and no more."

Dibble gave a backward glance. "The kid standing at the door, his name is Bobby. He's fourteen. I want you to take him first."

"Ahead of you?" She smiled. "Since when did you wait in line?"

"He's a first-timer, what can I tell you?"

"Four kids already had their hands up. What do you want me to do?"

"Drop one of 'em."

106

She motioned the boys forward and, her finger jabbing from face to face, said, "eeny, meeny, miney, moe. Out goes Y-O-U." The boy she counted out, on purpose, had holes in his pallid face from old acne scars and red welts from new disturbances. "Don't worry, kiddo. Virginia will take you."

Dibble sauntered to the doorway and leaned toward Bobby. "I got you the best. Her name's Sharon, the one looking at us. Take her to the room."

There was no color in Bobby's face. "I don't know if I want to."

"You got no choice," Dibble said. "Those are the rules."

In the room Bobby stood rigid. Sharon shed her shoulder bag and, with a toe to her heel, removed a pump, then the other one. "You scared, Bobby? Nothing to be scared of."

"I've never done it with a woman."

"Same way you do it with a girl. Ever do it with a girl?"

"No."

"Just little-boy stuff, huh? Not to worry." She traced long fingers over her hips. "I'm wearing pastel-blue panties, would you like to see them?"

He didn't dare say, didn't know for sure, and kept his stance rigid when she lifted her short skirt. Her underpants were little more than a label, which his eyes gulped up. She undid her skirt and let it fall.

"Never seen a woman naked?"

"Pictures," he murmured.

She had little more to take off. Unclothed, her body was an event. Her breasts quaked, her belly rippled, her hips expanded. Whipping her hair back, she said, "Well?"

He couldn't speak, not until she stepped toward the wrong cot. "That's Dibs's bed."

"I know. Let's use it."

He started to panic. "Did he say we could?"

"Dibs and I are old buddies."

She lay flat on Dibble's cot and smiled up at him. He saw her pubic patch as an abandoned robin's nest. When she parted her legs, he saw it as a monkey's mouth.

"Not still scared, are you?"

"No," he said in a dry voice.

"Your clothes, Bobby. It's better without them."

Slowly he began tugging, yanking, at one point tripping over himself. Naked, his face smarting, he shivered in the overheated room. Her smile grew.

"You sure you're only fourteen?"

"I'm almost fifteen."

"We'll cuddle first. Would you like that?"

He moved in the instant and was in her arms. Eyes closed, he breathed her in. His nose nudged her skin, and his fingers crept to warm places. Everything was solid and real and yet soft and dreamlike, as if two worlds, both lost, had locked together. She freed an arm.

"What do you want mama to do?"

He didn't know. Anything she did would be fine. His mouth found a nipple.

108

"So that's what you want." When she reached below, he spurted.

The history quiz, true-or-false variety, was easy. Bobby finished fast and sat back in his student chair, the paper on the desktop arm where Duck could see it. Grades on their papers were always identical except when Duck copied wrong.

Duck whispered, "Thanks, Bobby."

Moments later the teacher collected the papers and told the class to open their books to chapter twelve and read the first five pages to themselves.

His face in his book, Duck whispered, "It was good, huh, Bobby?"

Bobby barely nodded. Some things were too private to talk about. He had backed off even with Dibble.

Duck leaned sideways. "I had Virginia. She's always nice to me. Who'd you have?"

The name was too precious to come off his tongue, too sweet to release. "I had the best."

"Then you had Sharon. You lucky dog."

He had a vivid and sustaining memory of her arms around him as if she were shelter, though she was still not entirely real in his mind.

"Dibs must've got her for you."

"He let me go first," Bobby said and, lapsing into silence, closed his eyes.

Duck turned an unread page of his book and then leaned sideways again. "Whatcha thinking about, Bobby?"

"Her. I love her."

CHAPTER SIX

It was a winter when too much snow fell. The town went dumb with it. The cold made the snow seem like stone. It was as if the dead were being buried twice, Reverend Stottle said to his visitor. The visitor was Trish Becker, who had come to his house in a ski cap and full-length mink. She had removed the cap but not the mink. They were seated in a room with drafts. The room, which had a mood of its own, brought out the worst in the furniture, dulled colors, hid highlights, and resented the two windows. The windows overlooked the rear of the church.

"I can't stand shrinks," Trish said, "so I've come to you."

The reverend could not have been more pleased. He had little contact with residents of the Heights, who, if they went to church at all, went to churches in Andover, usually Christ Episcopal. "What's the problem?"

"It's Harry. It's his son. It's everything." She

pushed her hair back. "For the first time in my life I have a fear of dying."

"Are you ill?"

"Physically, no. Mentally, I'm a fucking wreck. Excuse the language."

Secretly he was pleased she used it. It made him feel more worldly without disturbing his spirituality. Indeed he felt his spirituality increase. "Dying," he said, "has a bad name, undeservedly. I believe that when the end comes we'll dissolve into music we can't hear while we're flesh."

"I don't see it that way. I see a hole in the ground, I see the dark." She stuffed her hands in the pockets of her mink. "Besides, you're missing the point."

He didn't want to miss anything. He wanted to help, to heal. His congregation he had endowed with a tribal quality. He was the medicine man. "What is the point?"

"Nobody can get away from what the kid did to that woman, possibly to two women, if the chief of police is right. His father is tearing himself up inside. Harry's an alcoholic, you know."

"I feel a grave responsibility," Reverend Stottle said. "I married you and Harry."

"Don't fret about it. I knew exactly what I was getting into, but now I don't know if I can deal with it. I feel like a coward."

Each looked up at the solid sound of footsteps. The reverend's wife entered with a silver service of coffee and slivers of cake. Trish accepted coffee but passed on the cake.

"You remember Mrs. Sawhill," Reverend Stottle said, accepting both coffee and cake, his sweet tooth showing.

"I've kept my own name," Trish said. "It's Becker."

"We don't see you in church," Mrs. Stottle said. "Of course we don't see much of Harry either."

"I'm a Lutheran. Lapsed. I can't speak for Harry."

Mrs. Stottle placed the tray nearby. Purposely plain, she wore a thick cardigan and no makeup. "That's a lovely fur you're wearing. Why don't I turn the heat up, Austin. Then Mrs.—Miz Becker—can take her coat off."

The heat raised, his wife gone, Reverend Stottle helped himself to another slice of cake. He was built bony and had only a bit of a pot. Trish kept her mink on but opened it wide. Filigreed stretch pants showed off the expanse of her thighs.

"I don't want to desert Harry," she said. "I don't want to leave him with nothing. I don't know what to do."

Viewing her thighs, Reverend Stottle experienced a sinful excitement he told himself he didn't want. A romantic, he imagined rapture in an idyllic setting, perhaps on a secluded bank at Paget's Pond. Fearing his thoughts were diminishing him, he said, "I sense a strength in you, perhaps a strength you don't know you have."

"Nice words, I hope they're true."

"Marriages are sacred, connections are everything. The world cannot exist with ampersands."

"More nice words. How do I make them fit?" She put aside her coffee cup, his wife's finest china, and crossed her legs as if, he fancied, for him to worship. She said, "I don't want the marriage to go under, me with it. I have to think of myself."

Nervously he contemplated a third slice of cake, the thinnest of the two remaining. No willpower, he gave in.

"Don't make yourself sick, Reverend."

Crumbs on his mouth, he spoke quickly. "I think you and Harry should get away for a while. Give yourself a chance at peace of mind."

"It's hard to get him to go anywhere."

"And I recommend Alcoholics Anonymous, strongly."

"He promises to go but doesn't."

Her voice was crusting over, which alarmed him. She was escaping, eluding him. He dragged his cushioned chair closer and openly admired her features. Her knee burned his hand. "I must work closely with both of you," he said.

"What?"

He gave her a deep look. His hair was wispy, hers blond and thick. His chin was dented, hers smooth and perfect. "We must all get in tune," he said in a hushed voice. "Before there was a world there was music waiting to be played, language waiting to be spoken."

"Are you coming on to me, Reverend?"

"Call me Austin." He imagined her elegant even on the toilet. "Yes. I mean, no."

She pulled herself erect. "I'll take your word for it. Whatever it's worth."

"Is she gone?" Sarah Stottle asked.

"Yes," the reverend said, standing behind his chair, which was back in its proper place. He moved to the thermostat and lowered it.

"What did she want?"

"She's afraid of dying."

"We're all afraid of that. Is she sick?"

"Her soul is suffering."

"Really," Sarah said skeptically. "I wonder how many minks were skinned for that coat of hers. She sure looked warm and comfy in it."

"It may not have been real."

"It was real all right. Why do people with money like to flaunt it? All it does is lessen the dollar and cheapen the merchandise."

Reverend Stottle, his head swimming, scarcely listened. His hand, still warm from Trish Becker's knee, had sensed the skin beneath the fabric. Sarah turned to the silver service.

"I see she tried my cake. Did she like it?"

He nodded. "She thought it very tasty."

"She didn't finish her coffee. Was that not tasty?"

He ignored the unaccustomed sharpness of his wife's words and smiled, though he resented her voice obtruding into his thoughts.

"For the life of me," she said, "I can't imagine why Harry Sawhill married a piece of goods like that. Wasn't he already living with her, more or less?"

"She's a fine woman, Sarah."

She turned slowly and gazed at him at length. "You didn't do anything foolish, did you, Austin?"

He colored faintly, just enough to show.

"Damn it, you did," she said.

Bareheaded, Chief Morgan felt the cold as he crunched over frozen snail tracks left by the plow. Snow was banked high around the green and heaped higher at a point beyond the post office. In front of the post office he saw the bundled figure of Amy White, though he didn't recognize her until he approached her. She wore a knit cap and a scarf pulled tight across her chin. Her nose was violet.

"I saw you coming," she said.

A gusting wind nearly threw her against him. He gripped her arm and steadied her, surprised by how small she was inside the bundle.

"We're leaving soon," she said. "No more winters."

He had heard that she and her husband had bought a condo in Florida and planned to live there permanently. "We'll miss you," he said.

"No, you won't. Nobody will, but before I go I want to know if it's true. Did the Sawhill boy kill my aunt?"

The question didn't surprise him. His suspicion had been rumored throughout the town and now was coming back to haunt him. "There's no proof."

Her eyes condemned him and made him look away for a moment. The sky was ice blue, the sun feeble. She said, "It's made me sick thinking about it."

"It hasn't made me feel good either."

"But you're the police chief. You have a responsibility."

He knew it better than she. He felt the weight, which had shifted into guilt, much more of a burden.

"I loved my aunt, Chief. I lost my mother young. Aunt Eve took her place."

The cold was getting to him. They each endured another hollow blast of wind that had swept across the snow-covered green, powdering the air.

"I'm glad I'm leaving," Amy White said. "I don't want to be here when they let him out."

"But I will be," Morgan said. "I'll be waiting."

Belle Sawhill picked up her daughters from Pike School in Andover and drove cautiously over winter roads back to Bensington. At the gateway to the drive she braved the wind and collected the mail. As she drove toward the house, the twins fidgeted. Jennifer said, "Anything for us?"

"We'll see."

In the warmth of the large kitchen the twins snacked on graham crackers and peanut butter. Belle sorted the mail. Ben subscribed to several magazines, which she put to one side, along with bank statements, one of them hers. Household bills she kept for herself to pay. The bigger bills were for Ben, whose secretary would tend to them. Advertisements and flyers she threw away.

"Nothing," she said.

Jennifer made a face. "You sure?"

"Positive."

"He never answers our letters."

Sammantha, refilling her milk glass, said, "I bet he gets lots of letters from people he doesn't even know."

Belle shuddered inside. She didn't want them thinking of him as some sort of celebrity, a special being, though she knew that among their classmates they now possessed an aura. "Bobby's sick," she said forcefully.

"I bet he didn't mean to kill that woman," Jennifer said.

"But he did. And that's why they put him away. To make him better."

"Maybe the woman was bad," Jennifer said.

Sammantha smiled mischievously. "Maybe she was trying to seduce Bobby."

Belle arched her spine. "What kind of talk is that? Nobody deserves to be killed. And the woman was a very good woman."

They lowered their heads, and she watched them crunch on their crackers and remembered them of an age when she still had milk in her breasts. Now they were ten, and their breasts were beginning to stand out like forced blooms. Too soon, too quick. It didn't seem fair.

"Her name was Charlotte," Jennifer whispered to her sister.

"No, it wasn't," Sammantha said. "It was Claudia."

Belle wished they were still toddlers chatting

away in unformed language, in the private syncopated talk of twins. When one had a cold, the other felt she should have one too.

Jennifer, her voice breaking, said, "He'll be all grown up when we see him again."

"We'll be older too," Sammantha said.

Jennifer looked at her mother. "Will he still be sick?"

Belle did tricks with her mind, worked it backwards, and said, "Remember when you two cut each other's hair? My God, you looked funny!"

Chief Morgan visited Mrs. Perrault. Guilt drove him to it. Mrs. Perrault's surprise was obvious and her pleasure genuine. "I've been thinking about you," she said, showing him into the overheated front room and seating him in a chair that seemed his now, or could be. "I was at the hairdresser's this morning. How do I look?"

Tinted, permed, and teased, her hair was a velvety mist, the hue reflected in her eyeglasses. "You look great."

"You never did come to dinner."

"I'm sorry, no excuse," he said and suddenly was back on his feet.

Mrs. Perrault's elder sister was in the doorway. Though it was midafternoon she was in a flannel nightgown, nothing under it, as if at her age she had nothing to hide. She swayed into the room and came close to him, her bust nearly in his arms. Her voice gusted.

"You have more bad news for us?"

119

Mrs. Perrault spoke sharply. "He's come to see me, Ida. Why don't you put a robe on?"

"I'm fine the way I am. I don't put on airs, and I don't need to impress the police chief." She stared into Morgan's eyes. "There's just the two of us now, her and me, two old widows hanging on."

He had heard that the younger sister had taken a spill on ice and broken her hip. From the hospital she had gone into a nursing home in Andover. "I'm sorry about your sister."

"She's gone loony on us."

"She's been diagnosed with Alzheimer's," Mrs. Perrault explained quietly.

"As if enough hasn't happened to us."

"Please, Ida. James is my visitor. Why don't you leave us alone."

"This is my house too, I pay my way," Ida said, but she left, indignantly, and clumped up the stairs, a relief to Mrs. Perrault, whose eyes had gone old inside her spectacles.

"Let's go in the kitchen, James. More privacy."

In the kitchen she served him hot chocolate, which he didn't think he wanted but found himself enjoying. He used a spoon to eat the dab of marshmallow floating on the surface.

"All this snow, James, I can't go to the cemetery. Do you go?"

"Whenever I can. My wife's there. Now Claudia."

They were sitting across from each other, Mrs. Perrault with both elbows planted on the table. She said, "None of my business, but were you and Claudia good lovers?"

"I like to think so," he said, taken aback only for an instant.

"I wanted so much for her to be happy. Her husband's death did terrible things to her. Now her death is doing terrible things to me." She produced a tissue, which she didn't use, simply clutched for the ready. "She has a shoebox of his letters from Vietnam. Should I keep them or burn them?"

"I don't know."

"I don't either." The tissue was crushed in her fist, an indication she was not going to use it. "Do you have a life, James?"

"My job."

"I have only memories. God gave us memories to taunt us when we're old. Old and ugly, but I was a pretty child. Grown-ups oohed and aahed over me."

"I can believe that. And you're not ugly."

"I never knew my real father, did you know that?"

Morgan said nothing. When he was a child he had overheard his mother repeating the gossip, which made his father chuckle, the sort of chuckle he knew was naughty. Perhaps that was why he remembered it.

"My mother had a fling," Mrs. Perrault said. "I'm the result. That's why I'm different from my sisters. They have the family face, I don't. I'm the oddball. My sisters have always known, but we've never talked about it."

Morgan said, "Did you ever tell Claudia?"

"No, but telling you is like telling her."

Morgan reached across the table and wrapped his hand over her fist. He had no words.

She said, "The dead don't grieve. They leave that for the living."

Moments later she walked him to the door, the tissue left behind on the table, next to the hot chocolate she had poured for herself but hadn't touched. When he opened the door the cold rushed in.

"You should wear a hat," she said.

He agreed with a smile. When he kissed her cheek her tears came.

"That boy, James. Don't let him come back."

A youth with dreadlocks and tan skin said, "Did you hear about Duck? He's a fuckin' hero."

Dibble, strengthening his arms in the exercise room, nodded. Everyone had heard about the outburst in Dormitory A, which housed boys fifteen and younger. A white twelve-year-old had tried to slash his own throat with jagged glass.

"Grissom was ripshit," the youth said with a laugh, "till he heard what Duck did."

While others were egging the boy on, Duck dived in and knocked the glass from the boy's hand but not before he suffered a slash across the cheek, the wound a flame shooting from his face.

"Grissom's giving him extra privileges and says he don't have to work the toilets for a month. It's all free time."

"He deserves it," Dibble said.

"You ain't heard the best part." The youth gave out another laugh. "He don't wanna leave the toilets."

Later Dibble and Bobby Sawhill visited Duck in the dorm. Duck was sitting up on his cot and reading a funny book, which he lowered at once, revealing a heavy bandage on the left side of his face. "Didja hear?"

"Yeah, we heard," Dibble said. "You're a hero."

"Am I really, Dibs?"

"You bet your Polish ass you are. Isn't he, Sawhill?"

Bobby said, "I wouldn't have done what you did. I'd have been afraid."

"I get extra dessert, didja hear that?"

"We got the picture," Dibble said. "Don't touch your bandage. Does it hurt?"

"Burns. They gave me shots."

"You're lucky you didn't get hurt worse. Why'd you do it, Duck?"

He looked stymied for a moment. "I don't know for sure. I think I didn't want to see the boy bleed. I hate blood."

Dibble looked at him sternly. "Stay away from the toilets for a while. Give yourself a rest."

"I can't, Dibs. That's my job."

He was back in the toilets within the week, restocking dispensers with paper towels and replacing rolls of tissue. At times he muttered aloud over the poor job done by the boy who had filled in for him. Mirrors were scummed. He was examining

123

buckets and scrub brushes and lining up jugs of disinfectant when Ernest sidled in and leaned against a sink.

"What's a hero still doing in the shithouse?"

Duck neither responded nor looked at him. He screwed the tops tighter on the disinfectant jugs.

"Heard about whatcha did. Real brave, Duck. What's your full name? I wanna put it on a plaque."

"Stanley A. Chmielnicki."

"You're shittin' me. What's the *A* stand for— Asshole?"

Duck drew a labored breath. He wished Dibble were with him, Bobby too. He wished his grandmother was still alive, her head kerchief-bound, her eyes loving him. Ernest edged nearer.

"Take the bandage off. Let's see if you really got a cut there."

He jerked back as if from a torch. "Don't touch me."

"I'll do what I want to you." Ernest hooked a thumb in the waist of his sweatpants. The hood of his sweatshirt framed his face. "Nothin' to lose, Duck. Another coupla weeks I'm goin' to the joint."

Duck's eyes burned with sudden tears. "I hate you."

"Hey, I want you to love me."

Tears brimmed, toppled, shaming him, but he found a voice. "I'm boss here. Get out!"

"You're nothin'." Ernest sneered, hovered, "You're just a fuckin' little Polack."

"Nigger," Duck said.

It was the worst thing he could have said, and he knew it. He wanted to reach out and pull the word back. He wanted to dig it out of Ernest's ear. Too late. Too late.

Ernest came at him.

Dibble came upon Duck an hour later. Duck stood unsteadily near the urinals, his eyes twitching, as if his mind were pitching and rolling. There was blood on the floor and some on his clothes.

"Jesus Christ," Dibble said, "what happened?"

Duck put a hand to his head. His legs buckled. He went down before Dibble could grab him. His head on the floor, he tried to smile as Dibble crouched over him.

"I fucked up, didn't I, Dibs?"

"I don't know. What did you do?"

"Ernest called me a Polack. I called him a nigger. I shouldn't have done it, huh?"

Dibble took a hard breath. "There's a difference, Duck. A big difference. You said the magic word." Dibble looked him over. "Where are you bleeding? I can't tell."

"I don't know. It came out of my mouth. I'm glad you're here, Dibs. Wish Bobby was too."

"What did Ernest do to you?"

"Everything." He reached for Dibble's hand. "Am I going to be all right?"

Dibble held him in his arms while he hemorrhaged. Dibble patted his head, nothing else he could do.

CHAPTER SEVEN

Harry Sawhill's face worked its way out of waves of sleep, out of other worlds in which dreams were only half remembered. Eyes forced open, he managed to smile up at his wife, who held a glass of orange juice, which he didn't want. His head stayed in the pillow.

"What time is it?"

"Nearly noon," Trish said. "Are you getting up?"

"In a while."

She placed the juice glass on the bedside table and noted his color, amber creeping into the gray. She raised a window to get the stuffiness out of the room. Mild spring air poured in. Turning, she said, "What am I going to do with you, Harry?"

"What will you do without me?" he said, producing a smile that surprised her. "Will you get along?"

"Depends. What do you plan to leave me? Your second-best bed?"

He closed his eyes. Drinking had gored his liver, but it was his heart that concerned his attending physician at Lahey Clinic, a woman named Feldman, youngish, bright, caring. Dr. Feldman referred him to a cardiologist, whose examinations resulted in warnings.

"Come down in an hour," Trish said. "I'll have breakfast ready."

"Just coffee, Trish. OK?"

Downstairs she phoned the Lahey, got through to Dr. Feldman after a short wait, and said, "I'm worried. I don't like his color."

"Is he taking his medication?'"

"Far as I can tell."

"Is he still drinking?"

"Off and on. More on than off."

"Then he's killing himself. Tell him I said that. Tell him I'm angry." Dr. Feldman went off the line for a moment. "I'm putting him down for next Thursday, three o'clock. Is that all right?"

"Thank you, Doctor. I guess you know he thinks the world of you."

"But not enough to do as I say."

Trish plugged in a fresh pot of coffee and stared through the kitchen's large bow window. Trees were swelling, leaves stretching out on buds like hands grabbing life. She felt none of the excitement of spring. Too long she'd been operating in a medium of vague fears, fears that were now gaining shape.

Back on the telephone, she rang up Ben Sawhill's private office number. When she heard his voice, she said, "We're going to lose him, Ben. He's not taking care of himself."

"When has he ever?" Ben said.

"I'm scared, scared."

"Well you should be. Longevity's a genetic gift, and Sawhills don't have it."

"Good God, why did I call you?" She paused to get a hold on her emotions. A bluejay lit on the windowsill and peeked in on her. The crest told her it was a male. "Ben, can't we do something for him? He's your brother."

"Tell me what I haven't done already and I'll do it."

"Damn you," she said. "What about me?"

"You'll go on."

"You guarantee it?"

"Not in writing."

Somehow his voice always cut through her anxieties and lessened them. During the trauma of divorce proceedings her children turning against her, his scoldings had sustained her. She laughed. "I do love you, Ben."

"That's something we'll have to discuss in another life."

Gently she pressed the receiver button down. When she blew a kiss to the jay, it flew away.

Someone was at the front door. With a glance at her watch, she wondered who in hell would be calling unexpectedly, no one coming to mind until the second before she opened the door. Reverend Stottle said, "I felt I should call on you."

"Why am I not surprised?"

"The last time we saw each other, I didn't mean to offend you."

"You didn't." She was amused it still bothered him. "I was facing a crisis and needed strength. I don't think you were the one to provide it—my mistake, not yours."

"I thought this time I might talk with both of you. I've never made a call to the Heights before. May I come in?"

After a hesitation, she let him in with a smile and led him over marble and then hardwood to the kitchen, where Harry was sipping coffee from a pottery mug at the table. Harry was in bathrobe and slippers, showered but not shaved. To the reverend's eye, he looked tubercular.

"What's the honor?" Harry said, blinking twice.

"I thought it appropriate." Reverend Stottle seated himself, and nodded gratefully as Trish served him coffee in a mug matching Harry's. His eyes admired the airy length of the kitchen and the hanging plants in the bow window. Then he concentrated on Harry. "You don't look well."

"They say I have a heart condition."

"Do you not take care of yourself?"

"If he doesn't, he'll die," Trish said, joining them. "He knows that."

Harry reached into his robe and scratched his chest. "I die, what's it going to be like, Austin? Angels to comfort me? Harps to play my favorite tunes?"

The reverend looked at him sternly. "You'll be deaf and in the dark. And nothing will matter."

"That's not what you told me," Trish said.

"My views shift. Sometimes I think the child we were waits for us." He tasted his coffee. "But I wouldn't count on it."

Harry cracked his knuckles, the sound like a mallet striking a croquet ball. "Tell me, Austin, do we suffer for a purpose? Or is it all for naught?"

"I've been having a problem with that question. I used to think it pleased God to see us endure our tragedies. Now I think it pleases him too much."

Harry did not look amused. Trish, who clearly was, said, "I'm starting to wonder who has the bigger problem. Harry or you?"

"I think God should be held responsible for defective minds and bodies and held accountable for his acts. For what he did to Job and Job's family, he should be drawn and quartered. And for what he did to you, Harry, he should at least be reprimanded."

Harry said, "You don't sound like a minister."

"But I am. A real one. God gave us light but for the most part left us in the dark. Though with some creatures he was forthcoming. I think a cow is born with the knowledge that man will milk her and one day butcher her."

"I don't think you're cheering Harry up," Trish said.

"Nor do I. I'm sorry, Harry. Tell me about your son. Do you see him?"

"He's written me off," Harry said aggressively and grated a hand over his stubble. His eyes were bright from an antidepressant. "I don't know anything about Bobby anymore. I don't even know who he is."

"Would you like me to visit him? Perhaps I can find out."

Trish spoke up fast. "I don't think that would be wonderful."

Reverend Stottle nodded with a sense of frustration. In other people's dramas he was accustomed to a bit role but was in no way reconciled to it. He wanted stardom but would settle for a solid part, his name somewhere on the marquee.

Harry's hands were trembling, which did not escape Trish's notice. A decision had to be made. "Do you need a drink, Harry?"

"Yes," he said.

Feeling the reverend's eyes, she said, "This won't be wonderful either, but I can't refuse him."

The reverend knew a cue when he heard one. "I'll see you another time," he said.

In June she drove to Connecticut to spend two weeks with her friend Gloria Eisner, who lived in a tony neighborhood that rimmed a bird sanctuary. During the first week they wandered twice through the sanctuary with binoculars, played tennis one afternoon, dined every other evening at the country club, and watched the latest video releases, delivery and pick-up provided. Gloria had seen at least twice every Jack Nicholson movie.

132

"He reminds me of one of my husbands, a real bastard."

"I don't like his looks," Trish said.

"They grow on you."

"I don't like my own." A bodysuit with yellow filigree gave her the look of a goldenrod in bloom. "It'd be great if we could choose our looks. Big catalog with lots of pictures. I'd pick better bones and be a legitimate blonde."

"What's the real problem, Trish?"

"My age."

"It's more than that."

"Then it's everything."

Gloria used the remote to lower the volume of the video, the softer sound giving Jack Nicholson a kinder presence as he caressed Shirley MacLaine. "Sad movie. I always cry, don't you?"

"No."

"You're going back early, aren't you?"

"I've been thinking about it," Trish said.

The next morning they were up by nine. Trish wanted a last stroll through the sanctuary. Focusing the binoculars, she confused a cardinal with a tanager until Gloria corrected her. Gloria pointed out a nuthatch, a sapsucker.

"Harry's brother knows birds. Harry knows droppings. Can you imagine?"

"Strange as it may sound, Trish, I can."

The sun swirled light through the trees. The relentless sound of birds and insects shook the air. The heavy beat of the morning took a toll on Trish.

"I didn't think I'd miss him, but I do."

Gloria gave her a sidelong glance. "How about his brother, do you miss him too?"

"That's an impossible situation. I no longer think about it." She fell behind Gloria as the ground rose and the path narrowed enough to have been made by goats. The woodland began to thin. "How did you do it, Gloria? You've been through three men, three divorces."

"They get easier."

"But a divorce is like a death."

"Then I'll have had plenty of practice when my time comes."

Trish felt a twinge in her back, a weariness in her legs. "All I know is that in my first marriage I wanted nothing more than to be a good wife and mother. I didn't do too well, did I?"

Gloria laughed over her shoulder. "I'm one to judge?"

"Let's turn back," Trish said, stopping in her tracks and consulting her watch.

"Don't you want to go to the top of the hill? You can see the whole town."

"I don't, Gloria. I really don't. I want to leave by noon and be home by three. I want to surprise him."

Holly Pride, the librarian, thought he was asleep. He was slouched in an imitation-leather chair in the reading room, with his head tilted to one side and a copy of *Smithsonian* in his lap. That was at two-thirty. When she looked in at four he was still there, the only occupant.

At the police station Meg O'Brien took Holly's call. "Slow down," Meg said. "What's the matter with him?"

"I can't wake him. And he smells. I think he had an accident."

"I'll get the ambulance over there. Don't panic, Holly."

Meg summoned the ambulance and then got hold of Chief Morgan, who was eating a slice of hot mince pie at the Blue Bonnet. When Morgan put the phone down, the waitress said, "I'll keep the pie warm for you." He reached the library before the ambulance did.

Holly Pride, alarm stamped into her face, directed him to the reading room and waited well away, near the copy machine, which wasn't working. When he emerged two minutes later, she said, "What's the matter with him?"

"The worst," Morgan said.

He picked up his car behind the town hall and drove to the Heights, to Ben Sawhill's house. No one answered the bell. Then he remembered that Ben and his family were spending a week in Montreal. Which left him no choice. He drove deeper into the Heights, to Trish Becker's house.

She answered the bell at once, giving him no chance to rearrange his face and prepare his words. He said, "I'm Police Chief Morgan."

"I know who you are. Where's Harry?"

"May I come in?"

She didn't move. She blocked the doorway. "If he's dead, don't tell me."

135

* * *

Mr. Grissom had a loose-leaf binder open on his desk, his personal notes on the boys. Dibble was in his office, also the woman Sharon, whose black mini with a lacy hem looked liked underwear. The subject was Bobby Sawhill. Sharon said, "He likes mama talk."

"That's not unusual," Mr. Grissom said. "Most of the younger boys do, and not a few of the older ones."

"All he wants is tit. I don't fuck, I nurse. Leaves me sore. I think I should get paid extra. It's like I'm doing double duty."

"Does he tell you anything?"

"Not much, nothing you'd be interested in."

Mr. Grissom scribbled in the notebook. The notebook was his third in seven years. In retirement he planned to write a book. So far Dibble was his prize pupil, but Bobby was becoming his most intriguing one. Inside the childishness he discerned the hint of cold intelligence. Turning to Dibble, he said, "How's he doing? Any progress?"

"He's taking Duck's death hard," Dibble said. "When I bring it up he gets funnylike. Doesn't want to talk about it."

"How about his father's death?"

"Didn't seem to bother him."

"I'd say not," Mr. Grissom said, seesawing a silver ballpoint between two fingers. "I could've arranged for him to attend his father's funeral. He refused. He give you any reason?"

"He doesn't like flowers."

YES! ☐

Sign me up for the Leisure Horror Book Club and send my TWO FREE BOOKS! If I choose to stay in the club, I will pay only $8.50* each month, a savings of $5.48!

YES! ☐

Sign me up for the Leisure Thriller Book Club and send my TWO FREE BOOKS! If I choose to stay in the club, I will pay only $8.50* each month, a savings of $5.48!

NAME: _____

ADDRESS: _____

_____

TELEPHONE: _____

E-MAIL: _____

☐ **I WANT TO PAY BY CREDIT CARD.**

☐ VISA   ☐ MasterCard   ☐ DISCOVER

ACCOUNT #: _____

EXPIRATION DATE: _____

SIGNATURE: _____

Send this card along with $2.00 shipping & handling for each club you wish to join, to:

Horror/Thriller Book Clubs
20 Academy Street
Norwalk, CT 06850-4032

Or fax (must include credit card information!) to: 610.995.9274. You can also sign up online at www.dorchesterpub.com.

*Plus $2.00 for shipping. Offer open to residents of the U.S. and Canada only. Canadian residents please call 1.800.481.9191 for pricing information.

If under 18, a parent or guardian must sign. Terms, prices and conditions subject to change. Subscription subject to acceptance. Dorchester Publishing reserves the right to reject any order or cancel any subscription.

JOIN NOW!

"What?"

"That's what he said, he doesn't like flowers."

Sharon glanced at her watch. "I'm on my own time now. You still need me?"

Mr. Grissom smiled warmly, appreciatively. He had tried out all the women in his employ to judge their suitability with the boys. Sharon was his longtime favorite, deserving of more money, but he paid them all the same fee. The fudge in his budget had to be reasonable. "No," he said.

Dibble remained, his manner cool.

"All right," Mr. Grissom said, "what's on your mind?"

"Still goes back to Duck. We all know Ernest did it."

"Ernest is gone. He's ancient history."

"You got him out of here fast."

"It was his time. Believe me, I don't think he's happy where he is. Duck's death was an accident. Let's leave it at that."

Dibble turned his eyes toward a blank wall. His T-shirt commemorated Martin Luther King. His sneakers were top of the line, a recent gift from Mr. Grissom.

Mr. Grissom sighed. "You say it was Ernest. Could we have proved it?"

"We could've tried."

"We'd have accomplished nothing except a scandal. That I don't need." Mr. Grissom got a grip on the silver pen and jotted something in the notebook. "You're my number one boy, Dibble. Don't let me down."

Dibble looked at him directly. "Something you should understand. I'm nobody's boy."

"Of course. You're your own man. Something I've been meaning to ask. Do you think Sawhill is ready for the dormitory?"

"No."

"I thought you'd say that. Sawhill still needs you, huh?" Mr. Grissom smiled slyly. "Or do you need him?"

"You sure we won't get in trouble, Dibs?"

"I got more privileges than you know."

They were sitting in the warm night on brick steps outside the building's main door. Beyond the fences peepers were shrill. Misted over, the moon looked like a wafer of metal covering a hole high up. Bobby Sawhill's eyes were on the stars.

"Do you think he's up there, Dibs?"

"God?"

"Duck."

"Why not? Good a place as any." Dibble gave him an elbow. "You're making me into a liar. I told Grissom you don't talk about him."

"But I think about him. That time I was sick I wanted to give him my watch, but he wouldn't take it. He said he wanted hands to tell him the time."

"You want to give it away, give it to me."

"You want it?"

"I'm kidding you. Keep it."

Bobby's eyes were still lifted. Slowly he lowered them. "Is Ernest going to pay?"

"Grissom says he's paying now, in the joint."

Bobby clenched his knees. Earlier he'd been sick, couldn't keep his dinner down, but he was feeling better now. He was about to speak when the big door behind them swung open and an attendant looked down at them.

"What the fuck are you guys doing out here?" He went by the name of Pete and had a mustache and a beard. Then, in the light from the door, he recognized Dibble and moderated his tone. "Why didn't you say it was you? Make sure the door's locked when you come in."

Dibble said, "How can I get in if the door's locked?"

"Don't be a wise fucker."

They heard the door slam. Bobby smiled, but the smile faded. "When you leave, Dibs, what will happen to me?"

"I got a while yet."

"I know, but when you do."

"You're going to be tough," Dibble said. "You do it right, you're going to be me."

CHAPTER EIGHT

The bulk of Harry Sawhill's estate went to his son and the token remainder to his widow. Ben Sawhill set up trust funds for Bobby, a special one for what he hoped would be Bobby's education, Harvard if possible. He considered selling Harry's house but decided it should be there for Bobby if he wanted it.

"So long as he never lives with us," Belle Sawhill said.

"He won't," Ben said. "Just don't ask me to turn my back on him."

Belle crossed her arms tight under her breasts. "The thought of him coming home petrifies me."

"You come first, you know that. You and the girls."

"I'll tell you who else is scared. Trish."

"She has nothing to worry about."

"Tell her that."

After learning that Harry was dead, the first person Trish Becker had called was Gloria Eisner.

Standing rigid with one hand in her hair, she said, "He's gone, Gloria. He's pushed off."

"I'm sorry, baby. So sorry for you."

"He might be happy where he is. Who's to say?"

"I'll come up."

"Hurry."

Gloria stayed with Trish through the funeral and two weeks afterward. Then Gloria brought her back with her to Connecticut, the visit considered indefinite. Trish phoned Ben, who promised to look after her house, and she called Belle several times, the two of them closer now than they had been before, with Bobby creeping in and out of the conversations.

"What will you do, Belle?"

"Cross that bridge when I get to it."

Sitting with a wine cooler on the patio, the day nodding off into twilight, Trish said to Gloria, "He wasn't someone I loved heart and soul, not like I did my first husband, but I cared for him. He tried to be good to me, but he was so vulnerable."

"My husbands were all vulnerable to one thing or another, usually other women."

"Harry wasn't that way. Poor Harry. I don't think anyone could have replaced his first wife."

They took more walks through the sanctuary. The air fluttered with pine needles. Colorful birch, maple, and oak spilled leaves. They climbed the hill where they could see the outstretched sky and birds in flight. Trish felt a sharp breeze through her shirt.

"Summer's gone," she said. "It was so swift, so unfair, so much like life."

When the sumac began to lose its blaze and the weather chilled, she said, "I want to go where it's eternally warm. Where I can show my ass on a beach. Where to, Gloria?"

Gloria, sitting sideways on a window seat in the sunniest room, was clipping her toenails. "Anywhere," she said. "As long as it's not Hell."

In Key West, Gloria judged the sun bigger and redder than in any other sky. Setting, performing for a cheering crowd on Mallory Square, it was luridly awesome, as if practicing to end the world. Trish aimed her camera, a Pentax that had belonged to Harry, but decided a picture would capture nothing.

"Poetry might," Gloria said, "but we're not poets."

"What are we?"

"Vagabonds with pocketbooks."

Shopping on Duval Street, Trish bought Christmas gifts to mail to her children. Gloria, childless, bought scenic postcards to write to friends. They dined on yellowtail on the crowded veranda of a restaurant, where Gloria reminisced about her great-grandmother who, according to family legend, had required her personal maid to bathe her after intimacy with her husband.

"She was still alive when I was a kid. I was allowed to kiss her on the cheek if I wiped my mouth first. My mother thought she might leave us something. She didn't."

"Harry left me practically nothing. I'm glad."

"Never turn your nose up at money. It's what gives you options."

They returned to the Casa Marina, the fortress of luxury where they had checked in a month ago, and slept soundly through the warm night and well into the morning. They spent the afternoon on the beach, which was not sand but crushed coral. The sun was blazing, the sky radiant, and the ocean a mirror without an image. Gloria allowed a young man who'd been flirting with them to rub her bare back with suntan oil but then sent him on his way.

Trish grinned. "Not your type?"

"Darling, he's gay. But he thinks we're rich bitches."

"Aren't we, sort of?"

"No. Rich is never having to worry."

In the evening they returned to Duval Street, which swarmed with tourists and exhibitionists. A man whose clothing consisted of a Panama hat and a bikini bottom edged by them. A heavy woman in the clothes of a child fluttered a fan in their faces. Jostled, Trish said she felt like a tropical fish swimming in the smallest of bowls. They dined again at the restaurant with the veranda, this time on snapper, the catch of the day. Afterward they went to a bar, but the music was raucous and much of the behavior bizarre.

"Not my scene," Trish said. "I feel uncomfortably overage."

"Speak for yourself," Gloria said, but they left.

They returned to the Casa Marina early enough for Trish to take a call from Ben Sawhill, who was handling her financial affairs in his usual fastidious way. "You're spending too much," he said. "You're dipping into capital."

"I'll slow down when I get back."

"Better slow down now. I mean it, Trish."

She let a couple of seconds pass. "I'm glad you're looking after me, Ben."

"I'm simply warning you," he said. "It could become serious."

Putting down the phone, she looked at Gloria and said, "You're right about money."

"Shit," said Gloria. "I'm short too."

Within the week they rented a small house behind Duval Street. A delicate fretwork porch that looked tentative fronted the house, and overhangs hooded the windows. Living next door in a nearly identical house were two middle-aged gay men, who took an immediate interest in them and invited them over for drinks. Barry, exceedingly handsome, was an artist who painted the human figure in fragments, the limbs adrift. Stirling, quietly distinguished-looking, was a tenured history professor on sabbatical from a university he did not mention. Both had gray hair, Barry more of it.

Barry served brandy in snifters. His paintings were on the walls. Intriguing to Gloria was a rendition of the Dead End Kids as disjointed cherubs. More intriguing was one of Mickey Rooney and Judy Garland as Adam and Eve, Adam's detached penis turning into the snake, making him the seducer, not Eve.

"Interesting supposition," Gloria said. "I believe it's true."

"Where did you two meet?" Trish asked.

"Here," Stirling said.

Barry took them into a bedroom to see what he called his masterpiece. It was an abstract of the sun imploding, time grinding into pieces, into a confusion of fiery shards and shivers, the past scrambled with the present, all of it stunning to the eye.

"Eerie in a festive way," Gloria said. "I like it."

"Critics aren't so kind," he said. "Shall I tell them what one said to my face?"

"Up to you," Stirling murmured.

"He said I paint dogshit and pretend it has thoroughbred meaning. A wonderful line, I must admit."

"And cruelly unfair," Stirling added.

Gloria liked them both, especially Barry. Trish preferred Stirling, whose reserve and dignified manner she found endearing rather than intimidating. Barry frequently invited them over for lunch prepared by Stirling, who made his own salad dressing, poppy seeds an ingredient. Desserts were custards, bits of orange on top.

One afternoon the four of them sailed on a small cruise boat to one of the islets, where Barry and

Gloria snorkled in the reef. Stirling and Trish stayed on deck and chatted about their childhoods. His, Stirling said, had been idyllic and more so as he grew older. Hers, Trish said, had had its ups and downs, nothing really traumatic, though adolescence, full of female upheaval and change, not to mention boys hitting on her, had been a bitch.

"Adolescence I could have done without," Stirling said.

Her smile responded to his. "Know something? I wish you were straight."

"No, you don't," he said softly.

Gloria's head popped out of the ocean, and soon she was climbing the ladder to the deck. Removing her mask, she said, "We saw a school of barracudas. Fantastic!"

"I was scared to death," Barry said. "She wasn't."

On the short ride back to the pier Barry and Stirling stood alone together in their swim trunks at the rail. Gloria whispered, "Christ, they've got better bodies than we do."

A few days later Stirling, who spoke fluent Spanish, took Trish grocery shopping in Cubantown while Brian sketched Gloria in the nude. She lay on a draped ottoman as if asleep, a hand behind her head. Brian did several rapid sketches from different angles and seemed pleased with the results, which he showed to her when she was back in her clothes.

"Some women have melons," he said, "you have pears."

147

"I was always jealous of Trish. She has melons."

"You and Trish are beautiful women."

"You and Stirling are beautiful men. You two seem very happy."

Barry turned away and placed the sketches in a drawer. "We put on a good front. Stirling is HIV positive."

Gloria felt a stab, as if it came from the back. "Oh, shit. I'm sorry, Barry."

"He won't talk about it, so don't you either."

"I promise," she said and stepped close to him.

"Hug me," he said. "I'm the one who's going to be left."

"I want to get out of here," Trish said when Gloria told her.

"Soon as we can." Then she began to cry, the tears angry. She had been putting away groceries. Peppers spilled from a bag. "I don't want to see them again. I don't want to look at Stirling. He's going to die."

"Not yet. Who knows when?"

"Don't you understand? I can't deal with it. I came here for the sun, not the dark."

"Trish, you're being unreasonable."

"Can't help it."

"We're not supposed to know, so don't say anything."

"Then why did you tell me?"

Two days later Gloria made excuses when Barry and Stirling invited them out for an evening at Sloppy Joe's, and another time when Barry suggested dinner at Fiorini's. The excuses hurt her. In the week that they were to leave she spoke privately to Barry and blamed the early departure on money.

"We all have those problems," he said as she read his face.

"But you're not buying it."

"Yes, I am. It's whatever you say."

"It's not the money," she said starkly, "it's Trish. I think she's in love with Stirling."

"Women usually are. I suppose you passed on what I told you."

"Yes, and she can't handle it. No surprise. One husband left her, and the other died on her."

"Then we won't say anything to Stirling. We'll let it be the money." He smiled and extended his arms. "Do I get another hug?"

"Only if I get one back."

When she returned to the house Trish was watching a sitcom, a bombardment of inanities. Her hair was pulled back and held with a rubber band. She was in pajamas, her toenails newly painted. "Don't say anything," she said. "I know. I'm a coward."

At the end of the week a taxi took them to the little airport. They arrived early and had a bit of a wait, no coffee available. Trish chewed gum. "I didn't say good-bye."

"I did," Gloria said.

Finally they boarded the airplane, squeezed into small seats, and listened to the propellers start to whirr. When the plane left the ground for the flight to Miami, Trish said, "Let's never come back."

* * *

From Connecticut Trish entered a lengthy telephone conversation with Ben Sawhill. "I feel I'm going somewhere," she said, "but it's on the *Titanic*."

"Financially speaking, you could be absolutely right," Ben said. He was preparing a budget for her, guidelines he said she must follow if she wanted to remain comfortably solvent.

"Why did Harry have to leave everything to the kid?"

"It was his call."

"I'm not complaining, honest, merely feeling sorry for myself. At least I came away with something from my first marriage."

"You came away with a lot. Don't blow it."

She carried the phone away from the patio and into the sun. Much rain had fallen recently, with trees propelling into leaf, greening overnight. "Gloria's in the same boat," she said. "Can you do anything for her?"

"Gloria's your business. Nothing to do with me."

"Am I family, Ben?"

"Yes, you're family."

"Your responsibility?"

"Don't depend on it," he said. "By the way, someone in the town was asking after you. He seemed concerned about you."

She laughed, her eye on the lowest branch of a maple where a cardinal burned through the leaves. "Not that silly minister, I hope."

"It was Jim Morgan. The police chief."

She watched the cardinal fly away, a live ember. "He was kind. I'm afraid I wasn't."

"He probably expected that. You're from the Heights. I told him you were wintering in paradise."

"It could've been, but the scales were tipped. He's handsome, isn't he?"

"The chief? Depends on what you call handsome. He's a widower."

"We have something in common. Tell him I'm fine." Following a breeze, she drifted ghostlike from sun to shade. Another spring, the green reinventing itself, which put a turn in her mood. "Ben, stay on the line."

"I can't. I have a client waiting."

"Ben, I'm coming home."

It was Bobby Sawhill's sixteenth birthday. Dibble and Sharon wished him a happy one, and Dibble gave him a slice of cake from the kitchen. Sharon gave him a kiss on the ear. Certain emotions were too much for him, and he looked away. When Dibble left them alone, Bobby said, "I didn't know it was treat time."

"Dibs arranged it with Mr. Grissom."

Bobby gestured toward the writing table. "I can sit there now. I don't have to ask."

"Terrific. You've got the world by the balls." She shed her clothes and helped him out of his. On the cot she spoke in his ear, the one she had kissed. "No more titty, all right? Mr. Grissom says it's time to be grown-up."

Bobby felt embarrassment and a twinge of resentment. "It's my birthday. Why can't I do what I want? Why can't we do what we always do and not tell him?"

"Because he's the boss and you're sixteen. You don't need baby ways. You're not afraid of me, are you?"

"I love you," he said.

She stroked his hair and ran a finger around the shell of his ear. "All the boys do, you most of all, Bobby. But I'm not your mommy." Her hand wandered down and made his part stand at its fullest. "Your mommy wouldn't do that, would she?"

"I was too little."

"But you're big now, almost as big as Dibs."

"No, I'm not. I'll never be as big as Dibs."

"That's all in your mind." She still had her briefs on. They were vaporish. "Take them off for me." Helping him, she lifted one knee and then the other. "Would you like to lick my envelope?"

He knew what she meant and thought about it. "No."

"Dibs does." When he didn't answer, she said, "No rush."

She fitted him with a condom, what the big boys wear, which pleased him. With coaxing she got him on her and with maneuvering into her. She swung her legs around him and locked her ankles. He began to tremble. "Go ahead, Bobby, you know what to do." He seemed stricken. His eyes were squeezed shut, his body taut, toes dug in. "Kiss Mommy," she whispered and broke the spell. Moments later he was gasping, and she was patting his butt. "Good boy," she said.

Lately, Bobby had been having a recurrent dream in which he teetered on what seemed the edge of himself, only threads keeping him from whirling off into a vastness that was inside him instead of out, a vastness where he would be alone forever, no Sherwood, no Dibble, no Sharon. He told Dibble about it and asked what it meant.

"Means you're fucked up. What else is new?"

"Are you fucked up, Dibs?"

Dibble snorted. "Would I be here if I wasn't?"

"You have dreams like mine?"

"I don't tell people my dreams. You shouldn't either."

They were in the laundry room. Dibble was running T-shirts, jeans, sweats, socks, and underwear through the washer, which was built for much bigger loads. He didn't want his clothes running through the same water with others, not even Bobby's, even though he and Bobby sometimes shared spit.

He said, "You got money? Get me a soda?"

Bobby always had money, a small monthly allowance from his uncle, half of which he spent on Dibble, sometimes more. The soft drink machine was near the door, Pepsi the only selection. He returned with one, glum-faced.

"I miss Duck."

"Sure you do, it's natural." Dibble took a swig of the Pepsi and shared it. "You think there're no toilets up in heaven? Sure there are, and Duck's in charge."

"You don't believe in heaven."

"I'm trying to make you feel good."

"If he's not in heaven, where is he?"

"Nowhere. That's what dead is."

"Yes," Bobby said. "I forgot."

An hour later, back in their room, Bobby sorted and matched Dibble's socks, and Dibble arranged them in his wall locker, everything in it neatly placed. A calendar hung on the inside of one of the doors, no days crossed off, no entries. In a dry voice, Dibble said, "Another five months I'm out of here. What d'you think of that?"

"No," Bobby said with alarm. "It's too soon."

"They're going to send me to a halfway house, get me ready for the real world. Neighborhood I come from, Sawhill, people expect to get killed. It happens, they got no complaints. Only the families do."

"I don't want you to go, Dibs."

"I gotta be a productive member of society. I'll work at a fucking McDonald's or a Star Market. Or maybe I'll work toilets like Duck did."

"Not you, Dibs. Never."

"No, not me. I'll get lucky and hit Megabucks."

Bobby said nothing. Finished with the socks, he began folding sweats, smoothing them with his fingertips, breathing in the redolence of detergent, a kind of pink smell.

"When I'm gone," Dibble said, "you stay away from drugs. They'll be trying to get to you."

"There's none here."

"Sure there are. Dorm C. Guys there deal. I protect you from them. I'm gone, you protect yourself."

"What if I can't?"

"You worry too much."

"You love me, Dibs?"

"I love me first, then maybe you."

"I love you first, I don't know about me."

A pillow propping his back, Dibble spent the next hour with his face pressed into a book while Bobby lay with his eyes shut, their cots no more than six feet apart, though for Bobby it was like an ocean. When he felt tears start, he stopped them. Then Dibble put out the light.

"G'night."

Without asking, Bobby left his bed for Dibble's and was not repulsed. Dibble tossed an arm around him. Strange night sounds came through the open window. For some reason birds were still awake.

"Ever wonder why guys here don't try to escape?" Dibble said. "They got no reason to. This is home."

CHAPTER NINE

It was a bad year for Chief Morgan. Investigating a charge of spousal abuse in the Heights, he tried to comfort the bruised wife and abruptly found her sobbing in his arms, which led to a relationship that put him in trouble with her husband, who was high profile, the ballplayer Crack Alexander.

Worse was a tangled affair with another woman from the Heights, Arlene Bowman, who wore crisp white shirts tucked into designer jeans that individually cost more than the sole dress suit in Morgan's closet. With her he was a pawn in a spiteful game she was playing more with herself than with her husband, diversion a high priority in her life, as if it were beneficial to her health.

His behavior caused talk in the town and was a favorite topic among regulars at the Blue Bonnet, their imaginations rampant behind his back. Randolph Jackson, chairman of the selectmen, told him to watch his step, too many rumors flying about. Meg O'Brien, shutting his office door behind her, took him to task.

"What is it, Jim? Middle-age crisis?"

That was in the winter. He hated winters. They wiped away gardens. The summer was worse. One of his officers, Matt MacGregor, died by his own hand, mismanagement of his gun, an unauthorized Magnum. Some in town believed it was suicide and accused the chief, though not to his face, of a cover-up. Malcolm Crandall, the town clerk, whispered that he was incompetent.

Kind words came from an unexpected quarter. Ben Sawhill stopped by the station one day, and they had coffee together in Morgan's office, the door closed. Ben said, "If there's anything I can do."

"I'm OK," Morgan said. "I tend to ride these things out."

"I wouldn't want to see another face behind that desk."

"Nor would I. How's your sister-in-law?"

"She's back and doing better. We all know what killed Harry. It was my nephew."

Morgan turned several pages on his calendar pad to bring it up to date. "Could have been the booze."

"Doctor at the Lahey said it was his heart, no surprise. It broke when Bobby's mother died. The booze held it together." The expression on Ben's face deepened. "What I really came to say is I hope there's no hard feelings. We had our differences over Bobby. We were all pretty emotional at the time."

"How's he doing at Sherwood?"

"Not bad, I guess. The administrator, fella named Grissom, says he gets into no trouble but refuses to take counseling. They can't force it on him."

"You sound worried."

Ben leaned forward and placed his coffee mug on the desk. "You were probably right about Mrs. Bullard. I think Bobby killed her too. The horrifying thing is we may never know why."

"I wonder if he knows."

"Maybe not. That's even worse."

Morgan reached into a bottom drawer of his desk and pulled up an unopened bottle, the cap sealed. "I don't drink myself, but this is twelve-year-old scotch. I stopped an Andover guy for speeding, and he tried to bribe me with it. I wrote him up and confiscated the bottle."

"Pour a little in my coffee," Ben said.

Morgan unscrewed the cap, breaking the seal. The taste of hard liquor had never appealed to him, but he poured some for himself too. "Cheers."

Ben, smiling, said, "I'm surprised that ballplayer didn't come after you with a bat."

"Don't think I didn't worry about it," Morgan said.

Crossing the green from opposite directions, they met by chance. A warm wind blew her hair back and gave her face more meaning. She was wearing a thick off-white sweater and dark trousers. Morgan said, "I didn't think you'd remember me."

"Your face," Trish Becker said, "is burnt into my mind. The face that told me Harry was dead."

"As I remember, you wouldn't let me tell you."

"You were trying so hard to be sensitive to the situation, and I slammed the door on you. Shall we, for a moment?"

A bench was nearby. They sat on it. A short distance away teenagers clustered around another bench. The girls, wearing Spandex, no breath for their bodies, chattered over and around their chewing gum. The boys wore ball caps askew.

"Remember when you were that age, Chief? My father defined adolescence as normal insanity. Do you have children?"

"No."

"I have a son and daughter, both busy being angry and misunderstood. My son should've finished college a year ago, but he took time off at his father's expense. Their father feels guilt so he gives them everything. They visited me in July but didn't stay long. They got bored."

"Not much for them to do here," Morgan said. "Young people from the Heights and those of the town don't mingle. They simply don't know each other."

Trish viewed him with her head tossed to one side, a hand on her hair. "Now that Harry's gone you're the only townie I know. I mean, besides Ben, but I don't consider him one. Do you?"

"I guess I do. Habit. Did you take back your own name, or are you Mrs. Sawhill?"

"I've always been Trish Becker, the name I was born with, damn proud of it." She watched random leaves rattle past her feet. A gray squirrel scampered across the walkway. "I have a friend living with me. She sold her house in Connecticut and moved in. A great way for us to economize. We're counting our pennies. Who lives with you, Chief?"

"No one."

"I heard you've acquired a reputation," she said and baited him with a look. "Arlene Bowman is an acquaintance of mine. I don't see what you saw in her. Sissy Alexander, on the other hand, is married to that beastly ballplayer. You must've taken pity. Am I offending you?"

"You mean you're not trying to?"

"I was testing the water. It seems clear we're in the same boat. We're looking for something, we don't know what. Does that sort of sum it up?"

"For you maybe. I don't know about myself."

They glimpsed Reverend Stottle, but he didn't see them. He was tramping across the far end of the green. Trish said, "Is he a townie too?"

"Not a real one, though he's been here long enough."

"The damn fool made a pass at me. Harry was still alive."

Morgan showed no surprise. "He's harmless."

"I've had it with men, at least for the foreseeable future, though I wouldn't mind acquiring a brother. Could you fit the role, Chief?"

"You have a brother-in-law."

"Doesn't count. I'm in love with him. Does that shock you?"

The cluster of teenagers was breaking up, the wind deadening their shouts. Couples with arms slung around each other headed one way, loners another. "How can it?" Morgan said. "I'm a policeman."

She was suddenly on her feet, leaves racing past her. Her hair flew across her face. "Some evening you must come to dinner."

He looked up at her. "Why?"

"So you can meet my friend. I think you need each other."

He dined at Mrs. Perrault's house, just the two of them. The elder sister had recently joined the younger one in the nursing home in Andover. "They're gone, and I'm glad," Mrs. Perrault said, serving him a pork chop, mashed potatoes, and peas. "I don't miss either of them, Ida least of all."

Morgan added gravy to the mashed potatoes and laid a sliver of butter on the peas. She had poured him a glass of milk, as if he were still a growing boy.

"Ida stopped taking care of herself. She didn't even bathe half the time, and I won't go into other details since we're eating. How's the chop?"

"Fine," he said, though it wasn't. It was undercooked, which worried him a little.

"I'll never let myself go like that. Thank God I got different genes." Her permed hair had a bright hue. Her appetite was good. With an accusing look, she said, "I've been hearing stories about you, James. I hope they're not true."

"What stories?"

"I don't care to repeat them."

"They're not true," he said quietly.

"Good, then I won't say anything more. You haven't said anything about the picture."

A crayon drawing of an elephant on manila paper was attached to the refrigerator door. He had avoided looking at it until now. "Claudia's?"

"She did it when she was in the third grade. I used to save all her drawings. I came across that one in the attic." A few peas fell from her fork. "I've often pondered where God got off making an elephant. I mean, what could have been going through his mind?"

"Maybe he was having a little fun," Morgan said.

"But at the poor beast's expense. That's not right, is it?" She glanced away. She looked old only at odd moments when her small jaw hung slack. "And why did he make twisted people? That's even worse."

"I suppose Reverend Stottle could tell us. I can't."

"I spoke with Claudia the other night. It couldn't have been a dream, it was too real. She asked about you, James. I told you were doing all right. Strange, she wasn't wearing her glasses, and her hair was different. She asked how I liked it. You think I'm going batty?"

He reached across the table and touched her hand.

"When that boy gets out, I hope I'm gone," she said. "I hope I'm deep in my grave."

Morgan returned his gaze to the drawing. The elephant was colored pink, its trunk raised as if to drink from the cloud drawn above it.

"Aren't you going to eat your chop, James?"

"Yes," he said and picked up his knife.

Trish Becker and Gloria Eisner attended a party in the Heights, at the home of the Gunners. Paul Gunner was obese from birth and filthy rich from the recent sale of his software company. The party was garish and loud, people from Andover and Boston adding to the mill. A five-piece orchestra added to the din. Paul Gunner's voice shot into their faces. "Enjoy yourselves!"

Gloria was a striking fixture in a tuxedo jacket and short skirt. Trish wore a silk dress that quivered. A man with a great head of hair told her he imagined her Rubenesque out of it. Stirred by the hot notes of rapid music, he tried to dance groin to groin with her. She pushed away.

"No thanks."

A man in a beige shirt with an upturned collar cornered Gloria and engaged her in quiet conversation, as if to establish trust, which went for naught when he began telling her of his latest experience on a water bed. Later she circulated with an eye out for someone who might be worth her interest. Only other women were candidates.

A man with too much to drink told Trish she was a wish granted, and she said, "Think again,

Buster." She caught up with Gloria and said, "Everyone's hitting on me. I'm getting bruised."

Paul Gunner was plowing toward them, couple of fellows he wanted them to meet. Gloria's eye was on the rise and sink of his belly. "He looks like a funhouse," she whispered. They got away from him, snacked voraciously from a platter of baked stuffed mushrooms, and then sought their coats, two minks among many. The cloakroom attendant was careful that they got the right ones.

On the way home, Trish driving, Gloria said, "What a fucking bore."

"There's still hope here," Trish said. "I know someone who might interest you. You should meet him."

"Does he have money?"

"Absolutely none, I'm sure."

"Then why should I meet him? Is he handsome?"

"Not so much handsome as refreshing," Trish said. "That's it, refreshing."

The week before he was scheduled to leave Sherwood Dibble came to a decision actually made some months ago and stored in the back of his mind. In the night he woke Bobby Sawhill and in the dark told him about it. Bobby didn't believe him, thought he was fooling.

"This way I get to stay," Dibble said. "You understand?"

Bobby felt a chill in his stomach. "You don't mean it."

"I ever say anything I didn't mean?"

"No, Dibs, never. Not the whole time I've been here, but don't you want to get out?"

Dibble laughed and slipped into his jeans. "What's out there for me? Name one thing."

"I'll be out too in time. We'll be out together."

"In here, Sawhill, we're in the same world. Out there we'd be in two different ones. You're white, I'm not. Here, I'm a prince. Out there I'd be dogshit." Dibble stood over him. "You want to come and watch? I wouldn't ask anyone else."

They padded barefoot down a long corridor to the toilets, Dibble in jeans, Bobby in skivvies. The silence was stunning. Duck's ghost stood by the sinks, scrub brush in his hand, a silly smile on his face.

"You see him, Dibs?"

"Yeah, I see him. Get out of here, Duck. This is not for you." Dibble opened the door of the storage closet and rummaged past mops and buckets for what he had stashed.

"I have to go to the toilet," Bobby said.

"Make it fast."

Bobby entered one of the stalls and, lowering his skivvies, sat on the cold open seat. He'd thought he had to go, but now he couldn't. He felt he was being lowered into a well and would have no means of getting out.

"Wash your hands," Dibble said when he came out of the stall.

"I didn't do anything."

"Wash 'em just the same."

"I'm afraid, Dibs."

Dibble was working a length of rope. "It's a kind

of slip knot," he said. "Guy in Dorm C showed me how to do it." Standing on a metal chair, he secured the rope to a steel fixture on the ceiling and gave it a yank to test it.

"You're not really going to do it, are you, Dibs? Mr. Grissom won't like it."

"This will tell him I've never been his boy. He'll hate me, but you'll be all right, Sawhill. Just remember the stuff I told you."

"What will Sharon think?"

"She'll understand."

"She's white."

"Next time look at her real close."

Bobby moved from one side of the chair to the other, a panic building. "What will it be like, Dibs?"

"Oblivion. Nothing more, nothing less."

"I don't want you to do it."

"It's what I want that counts," Dibble said, looking down.

The noose was around his neck. His stomach muscles were flexed.

"You got the honors, Sawhill. Kick away the chair."

"I don't know if I can."

"I'll do it myself."

Bobby started to cry. "Dibs, don't."

"If you can't do it, get out of here."

Bobby kicked the chair.

He didn't sleep. He lay on his cot and let the pain from loss embrace him. The embrace was comforting because it was familiar. Swept from his mind was the agonized expression on Dibble's face, as if he'd been poisoned. In its place was a false and peaceful one.

He didn't go to breakfast. Nor did he report to his job in the library. He stayed in his room until the attendant named Pete pushed open the door and said, "Grissom wants to see you. Guess you know why." He got into his sweats and sneakers while Pete smiled. "Whole place knows about it. Guess you knew first."

They skirted Dormitory C, from which a swell of voices rose. Bobby's sneakers and Pete's crepe soles muted their steps. Pete stroked his beard.

"We ain't had such excitement since Duck went out feet first."

"He's still here, some of him," Bobby said.

"Yeah? What about Dibble?"

"I haven't seen him yet."

When they reached Mr. Grissom's office, Pete turned away.

"You're on your own now."

Mr. Grissom was seated behind his orderly desk and wearing a shirt and tie instead of sweats. The set of his face was no different from any other time, except that he seemed more official now, his voice deeper.

"You were there, weren't you?"

Bobby stood with his hands behind his back, military style, parade rest. "Yes, sir."

"Why didn't you stop him?"

"He didn't want me to."

"Did you help him?"

"He asked me to."

Mr. Grissom's stare sharpened noticeably. "Some of us never should have been born, Sawhill. Dibble was one, you may be another."

Bobby nodded as if he had no argument with that, no quarrel with anyone, least of all Mr. Grissom.

"You and Dibble were pretty close, weren't you?"

"Sometimes we slept with our heads on the same pillow," Bobby said with a smile.

"I suspected that. He left me a note, Sawhill. I have it here. He said he wanted his death to count for something since his life didn't. That's a coward talking. He left you, betrayed you, you realize that?"

"No, sir. It wasn't that way."

"You're absolutely right, Sawhill. It wasn't that way at all. It wasn't a suicide, remember that. It was an accident."

"No, sir. It was—"

"You're not listening. It was autoerotic asphyxiation. Do you know what that means? It means Dibble was getting his rocks off and went too far. We've had that here before, we'll have it again. It's something boys do, *some* boys, not you."

Bobby wanted to return to his room and sleep. Sleep was a retreat. Sleep strapped him into himself, placing him where he had long ago been.

"The police will be here," Mr. Grissom said, "but there's no need for you to be involved. You'll stay in your room. If you're smart, Sawhill, you'll come out of this all right. In fact, even better. You want to take Dibble's place? You want to wear T-shirts and jeans?"

He wanted his head in a pillow, Dibble's.

Mr. Grissom planted both elbows on his desk. "Dibble was my eyes and ears. He let me know what was going on. How tall are you now? You must be six feet, and you got muscles. You don't have to be strong, just look strong. And always use good English. It sets you apart. Even better is you get to keep your room, no going into a dorm. You want the job?"

Bobby didn't need to think about it. "Yes," he said. "I want to be Dibs."

CHAPTER TEN

Chief Morgan was a dinner guest at Trish Becker's. Trish, with some help from Gloria Eisner, had prepared something fancy with sea bass served in a spicy sauce not entirely to Morgan's taste, though neither woman would have guessed it from his appetite. Dessert was a variety of sliced fruits, papaya and plum among them. Trish poured coffee into delicate cups that had the aspect of sea shells. Morgan feared his would shatter in his hand.

All were in pleasant moods from aperitifs served before dinner and French wine during it. The liqueur was creme de cacao, which they carried into a room where a fire was going, the log applewood. Morgan sank heavily into an upholstered chair.

"I'm flattered," he said. "I didn't realize I'd be the only guest."

"We wanted you to ourselves," Trish said. "We've never known a policeman, and certainly not a chief."

171

"Though you don't look like one," said Gloria, seated nearest him. Patterned hosiery gave her crossed legs the look of chased silver. "I'd have guessed an architect or an engineer."

"Not a townie?" he asked.

"Certainly a townie. You have that air of belonging."

He smiled at the two of them. "I feel I'm on exhibit."

"Good," the voice was Trish's. She wore dark eyeliner and showed cleavage. "Now you know how I feel when I have business around the green. The townies stare at me like I'm from another planet. And by the way, Chief, Reverend Stottle is coming on to me again. Should I swear out a complaint?"

Morgan sipped his liqueur, the taste coating his tongue. "Why do you keep calling me 'Chief'? James is fine. Jim, if you wish."

"I like James," Gloria said. "I've not yet met Reverend Stottle. Is he a local character?"

"Only a preacher with a thirst for the unknowable," Morgan said.

"Must be frustrating for him. He obviously wants to know Trish in the biblical sense."

Trish rose with a flourish, her dress animating her large shape. "I have things to do in the kitchen. I'll leave you two alone for a minute."

Gloria recrossed her legs. "It'll be more than a minute. She's trying to fix us up. She thinks you'd be good for me, which means I should ask you some questions. Are you of a gentle nature, James?"

"I've never known myself to be violent."

"How's your health? You look fit."

"Mentally, I have my moments."

"Teeth?"

"Intact. More or less."

The liqueur bottle, ornately crafted, stood between them on a miniature table. Extending an arm, Gloria refilled the little glasses, which sparkled into gems. The play of firelight on her slender face gave no hint of her age except to lessen it. "A relationship is bound to lead to sex. How are you in bed, James?"

"I've never rated myself."

"My eyes cross when I come. Like this," she said, demonstrating.

"Mine bug out," Morgan said, not missing a beat.

Her laughter pleased him, soft on the ear. Her voice was plummy. "Are you tipsy, James?"

"Aren't you?"

"Warmly so. Nice fire. If you had money I'd marry you."

"If I had money," he said, "I'd be hard to get."

When Trish returned with a tray of leftover dessert fruit, they were content with their creme de cacao, the taste of which Morgan was beginning to like. The fire held his gaze.

"Have you two hit it off?" Trish asked.

Morgan closed his eyes. "She's been teasing me."

"But he's been letting me," Gloria said. "He's a good sport."

"We need a good sport," Trish said. "A good sport who's a friend. Did you hear me, Chief?"

173

"James, we're talking to you."

He was asleep.

The mail had come. Sorting it, Belle Sawhill was horrified when she came upon a small envelope postmarked Sherwood and addressed to her daughters. They had long ago stopped writing to their cousin, and now, after all this time, he was writing to them. Trembling, she folded the envelope in half, unopened, and shoved it into her skirt pocket.

She was alone in the house, the girls still at school. No matter where they were she worried about them. They were at that awkward pivotal age, their bodies turning into events, their breasts noted for their early fullness. Boys were already phoning them, an obscene call now and then. Sammantha could handle it, but she was not so sure about Jennifer.

Sammantha was quicker in school but studied less. Jennifer, who applied herself, got the better grades. Sammantha kept a diary under lock and key, Jennifer wore her feelings on her face. A terrible tease, Sammantha could, if she chose, reduce her sister to tears but seldom did. Each was fiercely protective of the other. That protectiveness, Belle sometimes felt, was their weapon against the world.

Composing herself, she telephoned her husband and spoke in a clear rapid voice. "Bobby's written a letter to the girls. I'm not giving it to them, I don't care what you say."

"I didn't say you should," Ben said evenly. "In fact, I'd rather you didn't. What does it say?"

"I haven't opened it."

"Do it," he said. "I'll hold on."

She wedged the receiver between her jaw and shoulder and ripped the envelope open, a jagged piece of the flap falling to the floor. In her hand was a single sheet torn from a pad. The handwriting in the body of the letter was small and neat, but the signature was bold and big, unequivocal, manly in its sweep. It seemed about to spring off the paper.

"What's it say, Belle?"

She was reading rapidly and feeling sick. "He says they can visit him if they want."

"No way. What else?"

"He says he's a boss now, a big shot."

"He must be dreaming."

"Ben."

"What?"

"He says he saw Jesus on the cross. He says the cross was a rope." She began to cry. "He's really crazy."

"I'll call Grissom," Ben said.

Gloria Eisner, wearing a black sweatshirt and gray tights, came in from a run, which had taken her throughout the Heights, past all the grand houses, spacious lawns, and stone lions, and beyond, nearly to the Andover line. She pulled off her headband and let her hair fall loose. Her face was full of color. Trish Becker, glancing up from a magazine, said, "I should've gone with you."

"Yes, you should've. Tomorrow, OK? No excuses."

"I have to get off my ass."

"We've just agreed to that. Any calls?"

"No," Trish said. "Can't understand it. I was sure he would."

Gloria counted on her fingers. "How many days? Three. Four? I must've scared him off."

"I hope not. But I was right about him, wasn't I?"

"You weren't far off," Gloria said absently. She had brought in the mail and was tossing bills to one side and advertisements to another. "Two letters. One for you, one for me," she said, passing Trish hers.

Trish thought hers might be from one of her children, though she doubted it, and then knew it wasn't when she didn't recognize the handwriting. Gloria's was from Key West, the stationery of fine quality.

"Mine's from Barry." She read quickly. "Stirling's sabbatical is over, but he's not going back to teach. He's staying in Key West. Barry says they haven't missed a sunset, wishes we were there to share it."

"I didn't know you two kept in touch."

"I wrote him." Gloria smiled. "Stirling's doing OK."

"That's wonderful," Trish said abstractly. She was reading her own letter, squinting at the penmanship, though the signature sprang at her.

"Who's it from, Trish?"

"Harry's son."

"Christ! The killer kid. Why's he writing you?"

Trish tucked the letter back into its envelope and looked away. "He wants his father's Rolex."

"Give it to him. You don't want it."

"I don't have it. Ben does."

Trish rose from her chair and headed to the kitchen. Gloria followed her. In the kitchen Trish opened a can of peaches with extra-thick syrup, found a spoon, and began eating from the can. Gloria said, "What's the problem? Tell Ben."

"Yes, I'll tell Ben. Everything will be fine."

Gloria hovered. "That kid scares you, doesn't he?"

"Scares the fucking pants off me. Wouldn't he you?"

"Yes, he would. Are you going to eat that whole can?"

"If you don't mind."

"Get out of Bensington, Trish. You don't need to live here."

"You're right, I don't. But I'd always find a reason to come back. If it wasn't Ben, it'd be Harry's grave." She licked the syrup off the spoon. "Now you know why I want the chief in our corner."

Meg O'Brien told Chief Morgan to pick up, a call for him. The voice he heard was Gloria Eisner's, and he wished the door was closed because he sensed Meg was straining an ear. Gloria said, "You haven't called, so I'm calling. Does that bother you?"

"Not in the least," he said, keeping his voice low. "I apologize for falling asleep. I wasn't used to those fancy drinks."

"Are you a beer-and-pretzel man, James?"

He spoke louder than he meant to. "You want the truth? Chocolate milk. I've gone from Hershey to Bosco and back to Hershey."

"I should be wary. One of my ex-husbands was a chocoholic. Are you busy, James, or can you tear yourself away for a bit?"

"What have you got in mind?"

"How about a nice simple thing, like a walk?"

He chose the place, Paget's Pond. She knew where it was. Stepping out of his office, he tried to ignore Meg, who was giving him a choice look. As he passed her desk, she said, "What kind of conversation was that?"

"Private," he said, reaching the outer door. She said something else, but he ignored it.

Paget's Pond, ten minutes from the green and a little longer from the Heights, was past Wenson's Ice Cream Stand on Fieldstone Road. Gloria stepped out of a late-model Mercury still bearing Connecticut plates and gave a curious glance at his car. The edges were rusted, the town seal on the door faded.

"Shouldn't the police chief have a better automobile?"

"I take what they give me."

"Do you ever wear a uniform?"

"It has moth holes."

They moved into pinewood, past a NO SWIMMING sign, and followed a path to the pond, where frog spit lay on the quiet water. Farther out a breeze was skimming pictures. The breeze could have been warmer. Each wore a jacket.

"You're quiet," she said.

"How many times have you been married?"

She held up three fingers. "Scary, huh?"

"Children?"

"My unions were never blessed."

They followed the path along the pond. The sky was mauve, the sun subdued. Morgan said, "I'm curious. Why am I an attraction?"

"We like you. Isn't that enough?"

"I suppose it could be. If I believed it."

"Trish thinks we three should be friends. I don't think it's a bad idea at all."

A broken branch lay across the path. Morgan pushed it out of the way with his foot. "What's she afraid of?"

"Ah, you guessed that. You know what she's afraid of. Him. Harry's son." A smell of stagnant water wrinkled her nose. A number of crows, squawking mightily, flew out of the pines and startled them both. "He'll get out one day."

"That's a bit up the road," Morgan said.

"He wrote her a letter."

"Did he threaten her?"

"Nothing like that, but she's upset. We're two women alone. Trish would like to know there's a man like you we can call on. I like the idea too."

"You can call on me anytime. I'm a policeman. I'm the chief here."

"Why can't we all be friends at the same time? Is that against the law?"

They rounded a bend where they could see the whole of the pond, which had taken on a greenish

179

glow. Near the far shore the water looked clean and inviting. She took his arm.

"Why can't people swim here?"

"It's full of bloodsuckers and snapping turtles. When I was a kid I saw a snapper as big as a wash tub here."

"How many years ago was that, James?"

"Probably forty."

"And now you're an adult. Adults know that life is short. It's the price of growing up." She slowed her step. "Give me a small kiss."

"On the cheek or the mouth?"

"You choose."

When Ben Sawhill's secretary started to enter his office, he threw her a look that stopped her in her tracks. She backed off fast and closed the door behind her. He was on the phone, Trish Becker on the line, her voice deep in his ear, nothing cushioning it. "Calm down," he said.

She said, "Are you going to give him that damn watch or not?"

"He can't walk around with a Rolex. I'll give it to the administrator. He'll keep it for him."

"Just let Bobby know it's coming from you, not me. Christ, he's almost seventeen now. I don't want him bothering me, Ben. I don't want him writing to me."

"I'll do what I can."

"What are you going to do when he comes out? Tell me that."

180

"I'll deal with it then," Ben said. "Maybe it'll be a different Bobby."

"What are they going to do, shave his brain? I hurt, Ben. There's an awful emptiness in me."

He tried to be patient, understanding, but his head was beginning to fill. "We all hurt, Trish."

There was a significant silence. He was ready to hang up. Then she said, "Take pity on me, Ben. You owe it to Harry."

A few minutes later he was back on the phone, a call to Sherwood, to Mr. Grissom, with whom he was on close terms. A month after Bobby had gone to Sherwood he had made a thousand-dollar contribution for gymnasium equipment and more recently had provided the money for a twenty-four-inch Sony for the TV room. He told Grissom about the watch.

"I'll send it Federal Express. You can hold it for him."

"No reason he can't wear it, Mr. Sawhill. Nobody's going to take it from him. I run a tight ship, believe me."

"How's he doing?" Ben asked.

"I'm happy to report marked improvement. He's learning to handle responsibility."

"He's never written letters to us before. Now he's written two, one to my daughters. He says he saw Jesus on a cross that was a rope."

"I'll have to look into that. I wouldn't worry about it."

Ben ran a hand over his forehead. "Perhaps you

could divert any future letters, send them all to me. To my office."

"I don't see a problem in that," Mr. Grissom said.

Ben went into his private bathroom and shut the door. He took aspirin, ran cold water, splashed his face, and talked to himself in the mirror, in which he saw his brother's image merging with his own. His secretary rapped on the door.

"Are you all right?"

"No," he said. "I'm flushing myself down the toilet."

They drove to his house. Chief Morgan parked his car in the driveway, Gloria Eisner left hers on the street. They entered the house from the side, directly into the little kitchen. He wished he had not left dishes in the sink. She was amused by the jar of peanut butter and can of Hershey Syrup on the table. Climbing stairs, he wished the woman who came in once a month to clean had come yesterday instead of three weeks ago. She glimpsed a shirt hanging from a doorknob. He wished he had made the bed. She read his thoughts and said, "Don't worry about it." Her voice crept past him. "Where's your bathroom?"

"To the right," he said and hoped it was decent.

While she was gone he smoothed pillows and straightened sheets. He kicked a stray sock under the bed. In the dresser mirror his face was a stopped clock.

Returning, she said, "I looked into your medicine cabinet. It didn't tell me much. How much of you is true, James?"

"Fifty percent."

"That fits everybody."

Some of her clothes seemed to have wandered off. So had his chinos. The tails of his shirt hung over tapered boxer shorts.

"You have nice legs," she said.

Her bra was off. Her breasts were gifts he wasn't sure he deserved. He undid his shirt and she removed briefs that could have been spun by a spider. When she leaned toward the bed he glimpsed duckling fuzz in the small of her back. Lying on her back, she smiled.

"Stare if you like."

Her navel was a screw sunk deep, her pubis rust on a hinge. Her long thighs had heft.

"What do you see?"

A shadow divided his face. "Ghosts," he said. "Two in particular."

"Which am I?"

"Neither one."

"Good," she said. "Don't make me unreal." She beckoned. "I'm getting chilly."

Naked between the sheets, they warmed each other and kissed as they had at the pond. Her thighs parted lazily to accommodate his hand, which was not aggressive. Patient and precise, he had the finger of a jeweler nudging a stone in and out of place, which would have brought her about had he continued. Instead, to her annoyance, he rose over her. She was not fully confident she could enjoy him but soon found herself arching her spine. There was no frantic heaving. They harmonized, savored, and held off until the effort became overwhelming.

He rolled away and played dead. Speaking from the grave, he asked if she knew the time.

"I can't tell. My eyes are still crossed."

"Mine must be on the floor," he said.

She raised a reluctant wrist. "It's after five. Will you be in trouble?"

"I'm the boss."

His eyes stayed closed, but she knew he was awake. His breathing belonged to the living. "What do men want from women, James?"

"I don't know about other men."

"What do you want?"

"I no longer expect anything. Women I know have a habit of wandering off with me, vanishing." He shifted an arm and touched her. "I take what's given me. Gratefully. No questions asked."

She returned to the Heights and, famished, made herself a thick sandwich, Polish ham on rye, German mustard, kosher pickle on the side. She drew a bottle of Mexican beer from deep in the fridge and snapped off the cap. "You should see the house. Tiny. More Gothic than Victorian."

"Sounds quaint," Trish Becker said.

"Sears decor. Funny wallpaper in the bedroom." She swigged from the bottle, hard. "The things I do for you!"

184

"I didn't ask you to go that far."

She took a big bite from the sandwich and chewed angrily. "I never should have met him."

Trish looked at her knowingly. "You telling me you didn't enjoy it?"

"I'm telling you he got to me, but I'm three husbands too late."

Trish went to her. "Jesus, Gloria. I'm sorry."

Bobby Sawhill was playing Ping-Pong, slapping the ball back and forth, his opponent a newcomer from Dormitory B. They seemed equally matched until Bobby began exerting himself. Dibble had taught him the moves. When he chose to put spin on the ball his returns were deadly. Mr. Grissom was watching, waiting until the game was over.

"C'mere, Sawhill. I want to talk to you."

They went out into the passageway and ambled down to the soft-drink machine, where Mr. Grissom bought him a Pepsi, none for himself. Mr. Grissom was wearing new sweats, black with blue stripes running around the chest and a single one down each leg. He had grown a mustache.

"This is our world here, Sawhill. Out there's a different one, nothing to do with us unless we let it. What goes on here should stay here. And what goes on in your head should stay in it unless you're talking to me. You understand?"

"Yes, sir."

"Another thing, which I've told you before. Dibble did wrong, so don't you make him into something he wasn't."

185

"I still see him, sir. Him and Duck. Duck doesn't like the way the new kid's doing the toilets, thought I should tell you."

"You keep that kind of talk in your head. Even I don't want to hear it. Where'd you get that T-shirt, Martin Luther King on it?"

"It was Dibs's. I got all his stuff."

"Get rid of it. Fellas not your race don't like you wearing it." Mr. Grissom took the Pepsi cup out of Bobby's hand and drank from it. "Too sweet," he said and gave it back. "I have news about one of our alums. Ernest. Some guys in the big place taught him manners. Went to work on him with a knife. He's alive, but he's not the same."

"Good," Bobby said. "I'm glad."

"I thought you would be," Mr. Grissom said.

Bobby removed the T-shirt in his room. His roommate was a scared skinny kid named Jason, thirteen years old, with a face as dark as a coffee bean. "You want it," Bobby said, "you can have it."

"Gee, man, thanks."

"Don't call me man. Call me Sawhill." Bobby slipped on another T-shirt, plain, one of several his uncle had sent him. "You know who Martin Luther King was?" he asked, and Jason shook his head. "You come to the library tomorrow, I'll give you a book. I don't want a dummy rooming with me."

Jason quickly nodded. He was seated on Bobby's old cot. Bobby had Dibble's. Jason said, "Why can't we have a radio in the room, Sawhill?"

"You want a radio, go live in the dorm. Plenty of them there."

"Naw," Jason said. "I wanna stay with you."

Bobby did his homework at the writing table, none of it taxing. He read Dickens for a while and then turned out the lights, even though Jason was still up, reading a comic book. He soon fell asleep, but less than an hour later, in a dream, he heard a telephone ring and ring until it woke him up. He thought it was his mother trying to reach him. In the dark he heard Jason crying. "What's the matter?"

"I don't know."

When his mother appeared in his dreams he saw her as he remembered her, though with the texture of age added to her face. "You a bawl baby?"

"No!" Jason said.

Sometimes in dreams she fetched up his face and kissed his brow. "I don't like bawl babies."

"I ain't one."

He turned on his side and placed an arm outside the covers. "You want to come over here with me?"

There was a silence. "You mean fool around? Naw, I don't think so."

"Up to you," Bobby said. "No one's pushing you." A number of moments passed, and then he heard the slither of bare feet.

"I changed my mind."

"Too late," Bobby said and shoved him away. "I don't ask twice."

CHAPTER ELEVEN

Chief Morgan did not see as much of Gloria Eisner as he would have liked. She drifted in and out of his life according to her moods, a situation he accepted with argument. The last time he had seen her was when he was again a dinner guest, Trish Becker's invitation. Ben and Belle Sawhill were also there and seemed uncertain whether he was Gloria's special friend or Trish's. During dinner and after he talked more with Trish than with Gloria, who had learned that a friend of hers had full-blown AIDS. Apparently it was Trish's friend too, but Trish seemed less affected.

During a few moments alone together, Ben said to him, "I hope you know what you're doing, Chief. Either one of 'em could eat you up."

"We're all just good pals."

"Is that what you call it?"

Morgan colored slightly, as if he were in unholy complicity with both women. Casually he asked after Ben's nephew.

Ben said simply, "He's eighteen now."

At evening's end, Morgan managed a private moment with Gloria. His hand closing smoothly over hers, he told her he missed her. Light glanced off her metal jewelry, items she'd bought in Key West.

"Maybe you're just horny," she said.

He was on edge during intervals when he didn't see her. At the station Sergeant Avery's chatter annoyed him and Meg O'Brien's gimlet eye got under his skin. Meg, sensitive to his emotional shifts, said, "When are you going to settle down?"

His spirits lifted when his car broke down. He was cruising County Road when the overheating motor clattered, sputtered, and went dead. Felix from Felix Texaco towed the car away and phoned the next morning.

"Bad news for you, Chief. It shit the bed."

"A pity," Morgan said. "I guess the town will have to spring for a new one."

The selectmen, notoriously frugal with town money, were not pleased but reluctantly approved the purchase of a bare-bones Ford Escort, on which the bright town seal looked like huge postage. The selectmen arrived to view the automobile in the town hall parking lot. Randolph Jackson, who was no longer chairman but continued to act as one, said, "I still think we could've got it cheaper."

Orville Farnham, who was the chairman, said, "Treat it like it was your own, Chief."

"It is my own," Morgan said testily. "It's part of my salary package."

Two weeks later young Floyd Wetherfield, less than a year on the force, Matt MacGregor's replacement, responded to a call from the library. Elderly and cantankerous Dora Biggs, a widow, was causing a disturbance and flinging books around. When Officer Wetherfield arrived she threatened him with her cane. He drew his revolver. She dared him to shoot, and for a surreal second it seemed he might. Morgan arrived on his heels, suspended him on the spot, and took the heat.

Within hours Randolph Jackson strode into the station, Orville Farnham behind him. Morgan was in his office with his shirt half out. He stuffed it in. Confronting him, Randolph Jackson said, "Another officer playing with his gun. First one shoots himself to death, and this one's ready to blow away a little old lady. What kind of people do you hire, Chief?"

Morgan saw no point in reminding them that the selectmen were the final authority and had chosen Floyd Wetherfield over his candidate.

Orville Farnham said, "She could sue you know."

"She won't," Morgan said. "She had too much fun."

"What if this gets in the papers?" Randolph Jackson said.

"It's not the kind of news *The Crier* prints."

"I mean the *real* papers."

"They don't know we exist."

After they left, Morgan took a spin in his still-new car. He hadn't consciously intended to drive into the Heights, but there he was. He took a sharp turn into Trish Becker's drive.

Gloria wasn't around. Trish took him into the kitchen and served him coffee.

"You don't usually come calling unannounced," she said. "What's up?"

"I've had better days. Where is she, Trish?"

"Key West. Visiting a friend."

"The one who's sick?"

"The one who's dying."

Morgan toyed with his coffee cup. "She never told me she was going."

"Should she have?" Trish gave him a cynical look. "You two have the same kind of relationship I had with Harry before we married. Everything was up in the air. Marriage is better, believe me."

Morgan sipped his coffee. Some feelings he could not express and expected others to divine them and, if possible, explain them to him.

"Ask yourself a question, James. Now you know her, can you do without her?"

With Ben Sawhill's help, Trish got a part-time proofreading job with a small Boston publishing house that put out mostly self-help books. She did most of the work at home. On the days she had to go into the office she hitched a ride with Ben and occasionally manipulated him into taking her to lunch.

At the Maison Robert, where everyone seemed to know him, he said, "How's it feel to be gainfully employed?"

"I feel useful, productive," she said, "but I can't say much for the pay." She gazed at him pensively. "Do you know we're going to grow old together and never so much as hold hands?"

He abruptly stuck his hand across the table. "Go ahead, hold it."

Ignoring it, she said, "You can be cruel when you want to."

He ate rapidly because he was short on time. Tearing a roll, he said, "When's Gloria coming back?"

"When her friend kicks the bucket."

He gave her a curious look. "He's your friend too, isn't he?"

"No," she said. "Harry was my friend. I don't want to lose another."

Gesturing for coffee, he said, "How about the chief?"

"He's a shared friend, more Gloria's than mine, if you understand."

"The question is whether he understands. I'd hate to see him hurt."

"He's a big boy," she said with a tinge of resentment. "Order me a ricotta cheesecake. Screw my diet."

At his office Ben Sawhill looked through his mail, all of it opened by his secretary except for a gray envelope from Sherwood. Inside the gray envelope was a white one, addressed to his daughters, the first in a long time, ending his hope that there would be no more. He didn't open it. He didn't want to know what it said inside. In his secretary's office, his back to her, he shredded it. Facing her he told her he wanted a check drawn on his personal account, two-hundred dollars.

"Make it out to Ralph Grissom," he said. "Mark it recreation fund."

At day's end he was glad to leave the office. He picked Trish up at the corner of Winter and Washington, the traffic brutal, fixed most of the time. For a long while they couldn't get on the artery, and for a longer while they couldn't get off it. He gave Trish a sidelong look.

"As we grow older we should be less afraid of living," he said, "but that's not always true, is it?"

"The worst time," she said, "is when we realize we're utterly on our own."

With a slow movement, he placed a hand on her knee and didn't remove it until the traffic began to buck forward.

On Interstate 93 they didn't speak. He turned on the radio for the news. A basketball player of national note had been busted for marijuana possession. A serial killer was apprehended in Florida. The Congressional Budget Office reported that the richest in America were getting richer.

On the cutoff that would take them to Bensington, Trish said, "For a while there I was a port in the storm."

When he dropped her off near her front door, he said, "Don't read anything into it."

"Too late, Ben. I already have."

He took the family to dinner at the country club.

As soon as they entered the dining room, the twins, adorably awkward in high heels, became an immediate center of attraction, the pink freshness of their identical faces drawing admiring smiles. Their appetites were big. So was Belle's. His wasn't.

He felt a nervous exhaustion when they returned home. He soon went to bed, and Belle followed. He fell asleep fast and woke an hour later from a dream he chose not to remember, the chill in his chest a factor. Rolling toward Belle, he passed a slow hand over her body and woke her. His fingers plaited her sexual hair where it grew the thickest.

"What brought this on?" she asked in a sluggish voice.

He was totally honest. "I need to unwind."

Noontime, still in her robe, Trish Becker sat at her computer and proofed a manuscript about self-reliance and a healthy life through meditation. She didn't trust the writer, any writer. Writers were dreamers, and dreamers lived on air. Opening the dictionary to check a spelling, she gave a start when the phone rang. She knew without a doubt that it was Gloria, though she hadn't heard from her in weeks.

"He's gone, Trish." The voice was naked, raw. "He died with Barry holding his hand."

"You knew it was coming."

"I think Barry hastened it. A drop of something. I'm glad he did it. Stirling wasn't Stirling anymore.

There was so little of him left. Barry won't get in trouble. Officials down here are understanding."

"How's Barry doing?"

"He's running around, making arrangements, doing everything to stay busy. He'll fall apart when the funeral's over. Are you coming down for it, Trish?"

"I can't."

There was a silence. "You mean you won't."

"Don't be mad at me, Gloria. Please understand."

There was another silence, though not as long. "I do. I wish I didn't."

"When are you coming home?"

"No idea," Gloria said.

"He keeps asking for you. The chief. James. He's like a sick puppy."

"That's another life," Gloria said. "I'm not even sure it's mine."

She sat alone in a back pew in the empty church and drew a hand over her forehead. Nearly forty-two years old, she still didn't feel grown up. Sometimes in the morning, crunching cornflakes, she felt like an adolescent. Depressing was when she saw herself as an old broad. She turned at the sound of footsteps.

"I didn't come in to pray," she said. "I came in to think."

"I can't think of a better place," Reverend Stottle said. A look told him she didn't want him sitting beside her, so he stayed on his feet. "I often do this myself. Sit in a pew and mull things over."

"I'm down in the dumps, Reverend. I don't know which end is up."

"Fight the dark," he said. "Go for the light."

"I wish I had your faith."

"Mine occasionally falters. For an intelligent person, faith is a blind leap. Luck dictates where we land." He shifted his weight. "May I call you Trish?"

"Sure. Why not," she said, speculating on whether the two of them were more alike than different. "I'm a weak person."

"I have many weaknesses," he confessed needlessly, her shirt open enough to let him glimpse what he couldn't touch. "It was," he said, "either foolishness or cruelty that prompted God to make us as he did. He gave me the sensibilities of a saint and the balls of a billy goat. I have to live with it."

"Then how can you love him?"

"Loving God is like loving an idea. Except an idea is intellectual. God is institutional."

Crossing her legs, she flashed the lavish underside of a thigh and felt no shame. Why shouldn't she give a momentary thrill to a man in perpetual need of one? "A week ago a man I knew died miserably. All because—" Her teeth came down on what she was going to add.

"There'll always be misfortune. It's one of the vectors of life."

"I worry about Harry lying in his grave. No one to give him a drink."

"Our minds have a will of their own. When they want to worry us to death, they will. When they feel like misfiring, they'll do that too."

"Harry died because of what his kid did."

"No, Trish. Not at all." He leaned toward her in his collar and brown suit, the lapels frayed at the points. "He died because body and soul had had enough. His teeth were probably going too."

"Why do I want to spit in your face?"

"No one wants to hear the truth. I dislike it myself. It's like water unsafe to drink."

She struggled to her feet and stood outside the pew. He curved an arm around her waist to steady her. "I'm fine now, thank you," she said.

He walked her to the double door and opened the half that was never locked. "We all know there's another world besides this one. What we don't know is where it is, why it's there, and if we'll ever see it. It may not be for us."

She kissed his cheek. "You've made me feel better, Reverend. But not much."

She had a manuscript she had to return to the publisher, but she didn't feel like going into Boston. The morning was rainy, gloomy. She phoned Ben Sawhill. "I need a favor," she said, and he agreed to pick up the manuscript and drop it off for her. He arrived within the half-hour, the front door left ajar. She called to him from deep in the house, from the kitchen. He appeared suddenly.

"Where is it?" he asked impatiently.

She was not dressed. She was bottled milk in a gauzy gown. "Have some coffee first," she said.

"No time."

The boxed manuscript was behind her on the table. "You look haggard, Ben."

"I haven't been sleeping well. Not myself lately." He watched her pour coffee, a cup for herself and a cup for him if he wanted it. "You're not decent, Trish."

"You're seeing me as I am," she said and placed the steaming cups on the table. Raising her elbows, she showed her underarms "Look, I haven't even shaved."

"What are you doing, Trish?"

"It's all up to you, Ben. It always has been."

He followed her up the stairs, her feet bare, his shod. They entered a room in which the bed was in disarray. She raised a window so they could hear the rain. Out of the gown, she was ample breasts and blemished belly.

"This is Gloria's room," she said. "Since she's been gone I've been sleeping in her bed."

She lay flat, the covers down near her feet, and with the aid of a finger identified her scars, the longest the result of her two children, both by caesarean. He undressed furtively and approached big.

"I'm not used to the daytime," he said.

"It's supposed to be more fun."

He sloped over her, their torsos pale white and pink. "Do you mind being under? Or would you prefer the top?"

"Christ, Ben. Anyway you want."

He stayed as he was, deepened the fit, and became a prisoner of her legs, her twining grip meant to hold him forever. When his breath began beating against her neck, she got into the swing of it and egged him on. Her teeth scraping his shoulder, she sought his mouth. Without warning he broke away. Christ! He practiced coitus interruptus. No damn need for it.

"You should have told me," he said.

They lay apart with the covers half pulled up. She listened to the rain gain strength, take on power, and pound the roof. Some was coming in the window. "You're not romantic, Ben. Harry at least tried to be."

"I'm sorry."

"This was a mistake."

"Then you should have left it alone," he said.

"Yes, I should have."

He was out of bed, avoiding her eye, dressing as quickly as he could. He lowered the window. She reached down and pulled the covers to her chin. "May I?" he asked and used the telephone. Looking away, he called his office and told his secretary he'd been delayed and would be in soon.

"Some delay," Trish murmured when he put the phone down. "Will I see you again?"

"We've done it once. What'll stop us from doing it again?"

She watched him move toward the door. "If you're ashamed, Ben, we can forget the sex. We can just hold hands."

"We'll see," he said.

"Don't forget the manuscript."

* * *

Zipping up, Bobby Sawhill stepped away from the urinals and strode to the sinks. He washed his hands, splashed his face, smoothed his hair, and spoke to the mirror. Jason, occupying a stall, called out, "I know who you're talking to."

"It's none of your business," Bobby said.

Jason came out off the stall tucking a comic book inside his sweats. He wore Bobby's Seiko. Bobby wore a Rolex. Looking up at the ceiling, he said, "That's where that Dibs did it, right? Fuckin' hanged himself."

"Wash your hands. Use soap."

"I was gonna. You didn't give me time."

Bobby walked away from the sinks and pointed up. "Right there, *that's* where he did it. He's in oblivion. That's where you got no memory of yourself. You don't know you exist, so you don't."

"If he's there, how can he be here, you talkin' to him?"

"It's what used to be him that's here. And we don't say much. We don't have to."

Jason used an excess of paper toweling in drying his hands. "Where's that other kid? Duck?"

"They're together, but they don't know it. That's the way it works. Don't you have something to do?"

Jason was kitchen help, pots and pans twice a week, general clean-up the rest of the time. He said, "You want me to bring you back somethin'?"

"Cookies," Bobby said. "Chocolate chip if they got 'em."

They parted in the corridor. In the TV room he watched a show in which women abused by their boyfriends gave reasons for putting up with it. One of the women, light leaping into the lenses of her glasses, stirred a memory.

Sitting beside him was a Jamaican named Boy, from Dorm C. Boy said, "I like your watch. How much product you want for it?"

"I don't do drugs," Bobby said. "You're lucky I don't report you."

"You wouldn't do that, would you, Sawhill?" Boy's voice was mocking. He had an extra hole in his nose from the overuse of cocaine. "Besides, Grissom wouldn't wanna hear it. He wants happy news. That's what Dibs gave him."

The woman with the glasses failed to keep her voice steady and began to sob. The camera closed in on her and caught all the tears. The scene triggered more memories.

"Threatening me like that," Boy said, "I oughta whip your ass."

Bobby rose. He was bigger than Boy. "You want to try?"

Boy said, "Sit down."

Later Jason arrived with cookies, six or so on a plastic plate. He was wearing a borrowed jacket of baker's white over his sweats and had a big smile. "Chocolate chip like you wanted," he said. "They're still warm."

Bobby said, "Give Boy one."

It was treat time, but Sharon wasn't among the women, which confused him and deeply disappointed him. He inquired of Virginia and then of the other women. Mr. Grissom drew him aside. "I should've told you before, Bobby. She won't be back."

His face fell. "Why not?"

"She met a guy. She moved to New York with him."

"I won't see her again?"

"Probably not."

Bobby turned sharply and strode away, leaving Mr. Grissom to handle the women and their assignments. Virginia, who had changed her hair color from quince yellow to fuchsia, said, "You knew he'd take it bad."

"What I don't do for these boys," Mr. Grissom said with a sigh and tracked Bobby down in the laundry room. Bobby sat on one of the dryers, his big feet dangling, the laces loose on his sneakers. Mr. Grissom leaned against a washer. "She has a life of her own, Bobby, nothing we can do about it. I'm going to miss her too."

"She lied. She said she'd always come back."

"She told you what you wanted to hear, to protect you. You were her pet."

"She should've said good-bye."

"Something good comes along for a gal like Sharon, she's got to grab it. Think about it, Bobby, you'll understand." Mr. Grissom moved closer to him. "I've been putting this off, but there's something else we have to talk about. A few months you'll be eligible for a halfway house. We'll try to get you one near your hometown if that's what you'd like."

Bobby shook his head. "I like it here."

"It's not in my hands. It's up to the Department of Youth Services. They call the shots."

"But you got some say." Bobby slipped off the dryer and stood warily, as if people were trying to corner him. "Can't you help me?"

"Well, I admit you're an asset to me. And there's still the matter of counseling." Mr. Grissom gave him a wink. "Maybe I can work something out, but in return I want a solemn promise from you. When you leave Sherwood for good, you don't go the way Dibble did."

"I'm my own man," Bobby said.

On Bobby's nineteenth birthday, Mr. Grissom said, "You got a visitor. It's your uncle."

"Do I have to see him?"

"I think you should. He's been good to you. He's been good to Sherwood."

When Bobby entered the visiting room he saw a partial stranger whose tentative smile evoked memories of a caged canary, of baby girls with two women to care for them, of sweets eaten on the sly. Ben Sawhill saw a boy's face and a man's physique outlined in a T-shirt and jeans.

"You look great, Bobby."

Bobby said, "Is that for me?"

His uncle handed over a small wrapped gift. "Happy birthday."

Bobby opened it. It was a gold Parker pen and pencil set, initialed. Bobby snapped the case shut without thanking him. Staring into his uncle's face, he said, "You look a lot older."

"I feel a lot older, Bobby. Shall we sit down?"

They sank into plastic-cushioned chairs. Bobby slouched, and Ben sat erect with stiff shoulders and a barely perceptible tremor in his jaw. His voice was heavy.

"I'd have come long before this, but you didn't want visitors."

"Why'd you come now?"

"It was time. Your Aunt Belle . . . sends her love."

"She's never written. The twins did for a while, long time ago, but then they stopped. I didn't answer their letters. Now they don't answer mine."

Ben spoke quickly. "You have to understand. They have their own lives. They're busy with school, their friends. But I know they think of you."

"When they arrested me, why weren't you my lawyer?"

"I got you the best, Bobby, and he got you the absolute best deal. It could've been much worse, you know. Instead of going into a penitentiary, you'll be getting out soon. That's something to think about, isn't it?"

"I don't want to think about it," Bobby said.

Worry printed itself on Ben's face. He watched the pen-and-pencil case slip between Bobby's legs. "You should think about it. It won't be easy. A lot will be different, and you'll need to make adjustments."

Bobby looked at his watch, the Rolex, as if flaunting it. "Guys here," he said, "do what I say. They have to. I'm Mr. Grissom's eyes and ears."

Shifting his shoulders, Ben was aware of a weariness creeping through him. Nothing he could do about it. "I'd like you to consider college. I've looked into a couple of good ones. A friend of mine recommends the University of Michigan. Then there's McGill in Montreal. I have the literature. I'll mail it to you."

"I don't want it," Bobby said.

"You'll need to have a profession, Bobby. You'll need to earn a living."

"No I won't," Bobby said. "I'll have my father's money."

"How'd it go?" Mr. Grissom asked, rising from his desk.

"Not good," Ben Sawhill said. "He's got to have counseling. He should've had it years ago."

"He's already in it, Mr. Sawhill, but I don't know the value of it. He gives different answers to the same question. Most of the boys do that. They treat counseling as a contest, which is why I've never been big on it."

The tremor was back in Ben's jaw. "Something's got to be done. He scares me, and he'll scare me more when he gets out."

"You may be overreacting," Mr. Grissom said. "I think he has his emotions well under control. All the time he's been here he's never shown violent behavior. The closest he came was in the TV room, a minor incident, but it ended with him giving his antagonizer a cookie."

Ben was in no way reassured. Reaching into the inside pocket of his suit jacket, he withdrew the pen case and placed it on Mr. Grissom's desk. "He forgot his present. Would you give it to him, please."

CHAPTER TWELVE

Gloria Eisner stayed the winter in Key West and spent spring in New Jersey with her parents. Her father, a retired financial analyst, was battling a citizens' group that wanted to ban gasoline-operated lawn mowers in the town. Her mother was a pediatrician with an active practice in Manhattan. Her mother couldn't understand why she had sold her charming house in Connecticut.

"Money, Mom, no other reason."

"Don't you miss it?"

"Desperately."

Her father, with whom she'd long been on the outs because of her broken marriages, surprised her with a substantial check for her birthday. Looking at the amount, she said, "You didn't have to do this, Dad."

"Then give it back," he said.

Her mother said, "Why don't you live here?"

"Because I'd get on your nerves."

Her mother nodded. "Yes, you would."

She returned to Bensington on a weekday in June. Trish Becker met her at the door and threw her arms around her. "I didn't think you were coming back at all."

"I'm a bad penny," she said, breaking free. Trish helped her in with her luggage and in the kitchen gripped her at arm's length.

"You cut your hair. You look gorgeous."

"You look pretty good yourself."

"I've gained weight."

"Doesn't show."

"Liar."

In the evening they sat out on the screened patio with a bottle of wine and a cut of cheese. A breeze swishing through birches had the pleasant sound of waves lapping the side of a ship. The cry of a woodland animal had the quality of a child's laugh.

"I have something going with Ben Sawhill," Trish said.

Slow to respond, Gloria said finally, "It's your life."

"You think I'm wrong."

"It won't last, and it won't end well."

"I know that. But as you say, it's my life." Trish sliced off a chip of cheese and placed it on a spicy cracker. "I haven't heard from the chief in a long while."

"I've kept in touch. I told him I was coming back. I just didn't say when."

"Are you going to take up where you left off?"

"It's not a priority."

Trish gave her a cautious look and spoke

timidly. "Do you forgive me for not going to Stirling's funeral?"

"Nothing to forgive."

"You sound cool. Are we still buddies?"

"We'll always be buddies." Gloria drained her wineglass and lifted the bottle, an inexpensive Chardonnay, and poured more. "I love you, Trish, but in time I think I'd like to be on my own again. You know the feeling."

Trish refilled her wineglass, spilling a little. "No, I've never had it," she said.

"Help me, Chief," Floyd Wetherfield said. His year's suspension was nearly up, but the selectmen didn't want him back. Randolph Jackson said he should resign and make it easy on everybody. Standing before Chief Morgan's desk, he said, "They can't make me do it, can they?"

"I wouldn't take bets," Morgan said. "They think you're a cowboy."

"I've learned my lesson, tell 'em that," he said with a shudder.

Morgan felt sorry for him. He was an intense young guy, handsome except for a somewhat chewed complexion. A substantial head of hair covered his ears. Married, with a two-year-old child, he'd been working odd jobs, one of which was early-morning home delivery of the *Boston Globe*.

"What makes you think they'll listen to me?"

"You're the chief!"

"And they're the boss. Why don't you talk to them yourself?"

211

"I can talk to you," Floyd said. "I wouldn't know how with them."

After he left, Meg O'Brien looked in on Morgan and said, "Give him a break. We all make mistakes. You've made your share, God knows."

"Don't push," Morgan said.

"I don't, who will?" she said.

A little later Morgan drove to the country club and waited for Randolph Jackson to come off the green. Jackson's forebears had helped found the town. He had owned the woodland that was now the Heights, the sale of which had made him rich. He came off the green driving a caddy cart and climbed out of it pink-faced.

Morgan said, "Can we talk?"

"I bet I know what it's about."

Morgan followed him into the clubhouse, into the lounge, where they sat at the bar, near a dish of cashews. Jackson ate a fistful. The bartender brought him a bourbon-on-the-rocks. Morgan wanted nothing.

"He knows he did wrong. He says he's learned his lesson. I believe him."

"He's a loose cannon."

"He has a wife and baby. He gets back on the job, he won't jeopardize it."

"You think he's fit to carry a weapon? I don't. That's what it comes down to."

Changing his mind, Morgan ordered ginger ale. "He's working a bunch of jobs. Five in the morning he's delivering newspapers. He delivers yours."

Jackson wrapped a freckled hand around his

bourbon glass. His hair was sandy, a large bite gone from the crown. "You're blowing smoke up my ass. Feels good. Keep it up."

"You fire him, he'll have Civil Service fighting you."

"No he won't. He hasn't been with us long enough." Jackson smiled slyly. "You thought I didn't do my homework."

Morgan rattled the ice in his ginger ale. "Everybody deserves a second chance."

"Second chances add up, like the ones we've given you."

"Good ginger ale," Morgan said to the bartender. "Did you make it yourself?" The bartender smiled. Morgan spoke low to Jackson. "I remember the time three sheets to the wind you smacked up your Mercedes. I drove you home, nothing ever said about it."

Jackson swallowed bourbon. "And I got the rest of my life for you to remind me."

He was watching television when the doorbell rang. He answered it in his stocking feet. A wrapped bottle hanging from one hand, Gloria Eisner stood on the step like a flower with nothing greater to do than look beautiful. "May I come in," she said, "or are you going to shut the door in my face?"

In the kitchen he hunted up a corkscrew and produced two wineglasses that didn't match. He rinsed them out before setting them on the table.

"You knew I was back," she said. "Why didn't you phone?"

"I figured it was your move."

They carried filled glasses into the living room. The television set usually in the kitchen was plugged in near the sofa, where he'd been lying. Sections of the *Globe* lay on the floor. He attempted to tidy up.

"Mind if I turn that thing off?" She killed a commercial touting hairspray. "If it wasn't for fantasy, men wouldn't fuck. They'd watch TV." She raised her glass. "Cheers."

"Cheers." He clinked her glass. They took substantial sips, then sat together on the sofa. "I saved your postcards," he said.

"I got a thrill licking the stamps. They honored Elvis Presley."

"It seems you've been gone ages. Tell me about it."

"About Key West? It turned into an escape from winter. Staying the spring at my parents' home was to remind me I don't belong there. I spent a weekend in Manhattan and bumped into a woman I hadn't seen in years. She said the last time she saw me was with my husband. I had to ask her which one."

Morgan gazed at her profile. "I missed you."

"I thought you might." She let her head sway his way. "I've been untouched for all these months, James. I thought you and I might kiss and hug."

"Here or upstairs?"

She put aside her glass and kicked off her pumps. "We could start off here and finish off up there."

* * *

She was up before he was. Opening the back door, she gazed out into the smoky brilliance of early morning. Here and there, during the night, gossamer threads had been woven into little shelters on the grass. In the refracting light they looked like lost doilies. When she heard a dog bark from the neighboring house, she closed the door.

Leggy and languid in his pajama top, she was pouring coffee when he came down. "No eggs in the fridge," she said, "so you'll have to settle for toast."

"I usually have breakfast at the Blue Bonnet. I was going to take you there, show you off."

"Sure you were," she said and reached high into a cupboard for small plates. She had a splendid behind and didn't mind displaying it.

"I've died and gone to heaven," he said, sipping his coffee at the table.

"And I'm an angel." She buttered toast for the two of them. "I've not mentioned it before but you're not circumcised. I mean, most men are. You don't have to be Jewish, though two of my husbands were." She added peanut butter to his toast, not to hers. "I'm not complaining. I think natural is nice."

"Should I comment on that?"

With a grin, she carried the toast to the table and joined him. "I have news you may or may not like. I've decided to stay in Bensington for a while but on my own and not in the Heights, too expensive. A broker has been showing me places. I have my eye on one the bank took over. I can get it for a bargain price. It's not too far from the green. On Grove Street."

He looked up from his coffee. "What number?"

"Sixty-two."

"You don't want it."

She dunked her toast. "Don't tell me what I don't want. I'll want it all the more."

"Do you know what happened there?"

"Trish told me what you think happened there. It has nothing to do with me."

Morgan stared intently. "We're about to have our first argument."

Trish Becker stepped off the curb at Winter and Washington, slipped into Ben Sawhill's comfortable car, shoved her newly acquired briefcase in back, and strapped herself in. Ben twisted the car back into traffic. "Good day?" he asked.

"Sort of." She loosened the skirt of her suit, which had been pinching, the zipper at fault. "I met Lula Simmons."

"Who's Lula Simmons?"

"She wrote those two books: *Speaking Fatly* when she was in her twenties and *Speaking Thinly* after she had trimmed herself with diet and exercise. I'm proofing her third, *Speaking Honestly,* about her struggle as a woman."

"Sounds interesting," Ben said unconvincingly.

Trish lowered her window as they inched toward Government Center. The traffic took on an odd beat, like an orchestra tuning up. Pigeons swirled up from the mall like packages coming apart.

"Neither of her marriages were successful," Trish said. "Bummers, both. She said she never made love with either husband. She merely copulated with them and produced two sets of children, the second set less ungrateful than the first."

"Maybe she never met the right man," Ben said.

"The right man never met her. She says he probably resides in Finland or Tibet, which makes a meeting unlikely."

Bus fumes made her raise the window. Ben angled toward the artery, and they got on it sooner than they'd thought, though Trish was in no hurry.

"She's seeing a younger man, but she says only raw nerves, hers, and sexual energy, his, keeps the affair going. It's all in the book."

"Are you asking me to read it?"

"No. You wouldn't like it." She lowered the window again.

"What's the use of air-conditioning if you keep doing that?"

"None at all. Lula says her second husband was an industrial polluter, which made him a human turd."

"Enough, Trish."

Traffic rolled free off the artery onto the interstate. The sky opened up, revealing a large cloud shaped like the torso of a woman. It made her look twice.

"Any chance of seeing you later?"

"None," he said. "Belle and I are going out."

Trish dropped her head back. They were in a middle lane. Cars whizzed by on each side. "Have you noticed, Ben, we always screw in silence. We never say a word."

Ben kept his eyes on the road. "Is that a time for conversation?"

"Are you silent with Belle?"

"Drop it," he said in a deathly quiet voice.

Neither spoke during the rest of the drive. On Ruskin Road, which led to the Heights, they interrupted crows scrapping over carrion. When he pulled the car up near her front door, she unharnessed herself and patted his thigh.

"It's all right, Ben. I still love you."

The twins were watching television, eating popcorn, drinking Coca-Cola. Each was sitting on the floor against propped cushions, each wearing cutoff jerseys and shorts, their midriffs exposed. At fourteen, nearly fifteen, their bodies were accumulated treasures, the value obvious when they were in the company of boys. Jennifer was shy and aloof. Sammantha had two youths calling her, Mark English, who was overly handsome and saw Hollywood in his future, and Russ Lapierre, who was not handsome at all but had a way about him.

"I don't understand what you see in either of them," Jennifer said.

"It's not like I'm serious about either of 'em," Sammantha said and gave her sister a shrewd look. "They're like the rest. You know."

"No, tell me."

"They all want you to touch it. If you don't, they call you a goody-goody."

Jennifer took a quick swig of Coke. "Have you ever touched it?"

"Once," Sammantha said. "No big deal."

Jennifer grimaced. "I'd never do that."

"It doesn't bite." Sammantha had the remote and changed the channel.

"I was watching that!"

"It was boring."

"Sam, what does it do?"

"Spurts."

"Cripes!"

Sammantha changed the channel again, the sound increasing because of a commercial. Dog food was the product.

"Sam, what if . . ."

"It has to be in you." She switched back to the channel they were originally watching, the laugh track in full force. "I was just thinking, Bobby will be getting out soon. He won't recognize us, I bet."

"I don't know if I want to see him," Jennifer said. "I heard it was really *two* women he killed."

"That's just a rumor."

"What if it isn't?"

"Then it's true, nothing we can do about it."

Jennifer ran her fingers into the bowl of popcorn but didn't pick up any. "What will you say when you see him?"

"He's our cousin. I'll say hi and give him a kiss."

Jennifer stared at the television screen, a sitcom,

and saw none of it. "If one of us died, Sam, what would the other one do?"

Sammantha threw her a startled look. "What did you ask that for?"

"You know why. Bobby."

On the drive home from Cinema Showcase in Lawrence, Belle Sawhill said, "When he's back, will we dare leave the girls alone?"

Ben stared straight ahead, both hands on the wheel. "Why would he want to hurt them?"

"I don't know. Why did he kill Claudia MacLeod? We don't know that either. And Mrs. Bullard. There's another unknown. Lots of things we don't know, Ben."

The lights of an approaching car flashed bright because Ben had neglected to lower his.

"I think we should move out of Bensington," she said. "It's not the same anymore. He's changed everything."

"We can't let him do this to our lives. Where would we go? To another part of the state? Another part of the country? No, Belle, it wouldn't solve anything."

Another car hurled its lights at them.

"Will you dim your fucking lights, please!"

He did. "Belle, calm down."

She took some deep breaths. "So what are we going to do?"

"We'll deal with it, somehow. Trust me."

She looked away. "No, Ben. I'm afraid I don't."

* * *

Chief Morgan viewed it from the street. A few shingles were sliding off the roof, slats escaping blinds, paint vanishing from the sun side. He tailed Gloria Eisner through the low gateway. The flower garden was weeds. Rose bushes had turned wild, some looked vicious.

"I know it needs work," Gloria said. "That's one of the reasons I got it cheap."

Morgan said, "A purchase agreement doesn't mean you have to go through with it. You can get your money back."

"I don't want my money back, I want the house. I want to make it mine. I love that little balcony, don't you?"

"It could fall off," he said, mounting the steps with her. He pushed a button. The doorbell was failing, the ring of a faint stutter.

"You expecting someone to answer, James?"

"Just testing it."

"The young couple living here separated and walked away from it. The bank gave me a key."

When she opened the door and stepped in, Morgan drew back. "I don't care to go in," he said, and she stared out at him. He frowned. "I've seen death in it. Two times. Two women."

"Will you never come in?"

"I don't know. It may take awhile."

"I estimate it'll be a couple of months before I can move in. Will that be time enough?"

He moved forward a bit and looked into her eyes. "Change your mind."

"It would be healthier if you did," she said.

221

* * *

Reverend Stottle carried two coffees from the Blue Bonnet onto the green and presented one to Trish Becker, who'd been waiting for him on a bench, her attention fixed on a towering red maple. Leaves were breaking loose from branches and taking flight. "Summer's gone," she said. "It forgot to say good-bye."

Settling beside her, Reverend Stottle enjoyed the closeness. When she glanced at him through dark glasses, he viewed himself in the lenses. "When I was a boy I looked forward to autumn, loved the smell of burning leaves. Now it's outlawed."

"I want them to stay where they belong. On the tree."

"A leaf turns and a rose withers because God demands it. He demands it of every living thing, even of himself. Like stars that die but still shed light, he may already be gone. He may even have left before we began."

Her coffee had sugar in it, but she didn't complain. She said, "Life is tough, isn't it?"

Reverend Stottle liked sugar and had extra in his. "Living requires courage, fortitude, and from time to time a good stiff drink. Indulging in the latter can make you an alcoholic. God knows we don't want you ending up like Harry."

"Sometimes I think I'm going crazy."

"What a coincidence. I have that feeling each day."

She dumped some of her coffee out to prevent spilling it, then spoke vulnerably, as if reduced to her underwear. "Ben and I are fucking. How wrong is it?"

He raised his eyes and thought carefully. "The sex act takes its cue from the to-and-fro motion of molecules, the molecules that keep our world intact, that keep us from falling apart. Seen another way, woman is the inclined plane and man the lever, the rigid bar that transmits force. Everything is physics. Maybe God put us into play, but my private opinion is that he's long gone. Otherwise he'd be refereeing."

"What the hell are you saying, Reverend? You're not answering my question."

"I'm saying that if getting it off with Ben Sawhill keeps you whole, how can it be wrong? If, on the other hand, it's tearing you apart, how can it be right?"

She studied the smudge of lipstick on the edge of her coffee cup. "I'm so confused."

"It's the human condition. Otherwise men and women would have no need of each other."

She placed the cup on the bench and stood up. He rose at the same time. "I don't know how much it has helped," she said, "but I'm glad we talked."

"Call on me anytime. Day or night," he added.

She would have stepped closer and kissed his cheek, but his erection, straining thin trousers, was in the way. She pictured it as the tongue of a church bell. She shook his hand. "Thank you," she said.

* * *

223

Officer Floyd Wetherfield appeared in Chief Morgan's office in full uniform, with tears in his eyes and his wife at his side. "We both come to thank you, Chief." He flung an arm around his wife. "Tell him what it means to me, Betty."

"It means everything." Betty, a bit of a thing, had a high voice and an uncommonly pretty face of apple pink. "Now he can hold his head up."

"I won't have to sling newspapers at doorsteps."

"I used to help him stuff 'em in plastic sleeves when it rained."

"You must've missed one. Mine came wet the other day." Morgan tipped back in his chair. "If you screw up again, Floyd, it'll be my neck as well as yours. You understand that?"

"He does," Betty said.

"I do."

Morgan softened his expression. "Who's minding the baby?"

"My mother," Betty said.

"We have another son, we're gonna name him James. We've already decided, haven't we, honey?"

She nodded. "We love you, Chief."

"You don't have to go that far," Morgan said and picked up the telephone in the pretense of using it. "OK, I'll see you two later. You have a shift coming up, Floyd."

They shuffled out, Officer Wetherfield leading his wife by the hand, but a second later he popped his head back in as Morgan was putting the phone down. "I owe you, Chief."

"Yes, you do, Floyd."

A little later, all smiles, Meg O'Brien rambled in, came around his desk, and rumpled his hair, something she had not done in years. "Don't you feel nice inside now?"

"No," he said, "I feel I'm out on a limb."

Trish Becker was toiling over a manuscript when the doorbell rang. The midmorning visitor was Belle Sawhill. Her black hair brushed severely to one side, Belle was wearing a trench coat, which she kept on. Trish wore a fisherman's sweater, jeans, athletic socks, and no shoes.

"Coffee, Belle?"

"Nothing." Belle sat at the table, her shoulders straight, her hands in her coat pockets, and gazed at the manuscript. "Ben got you this job, didn't he?"

"Yes."

A cigarette burned in an ashtray. Others had quit smoking, Trish had taken it up. She put the cigarette out. Belle's eyes ground into her.

"You got your way, didn't you?"

She flinched and didn't try to deny anything. "What did Ben tell you?"

"He didn't tell me anything, but did you think I wouldn't guess?"

"Belle, I'm sorry."

Belle seemed offended by the apology, and the air hardened between them. "It doesn't excuse him, but you took advantage."

"I did."

"Break it off," Belle said, her voice full of weight.

"He'll soon be doing that himself. I can feel it coming."

"The sooner the better. For all of us." Belle rose. "Should I tell him you've been here?"

"You do as you like."

Trish walked her to the door and paused before opening it. "I do love him. Pity he doesn't love me."

Belle's face was blank and drawn. "More of a pity you don't love yourself."

Both hands on the wheel, Ben Sawhill kept to the left, eased onto the Interstate, and immediately picked up speed. Trish, her head thrown back and her eyes closed, said, "They want me full-time. They want to make me an editor."

Ben switched to the passing lane. "Grab it."

"I intend to."

They said nothing more until they reached Bensington. He mentioned his dislike of November. No finish on its surface. No tapestry on its walls.

"December's no fun either," she said.

He sped up the drive to her house and came to a swift stop. She reached in the back for her briefcase. His fingers played on the steering wheel.

"It's over, isn't it, Ben?"

He nodded.

She said, "Good."

Bobby Sawhill and Mr. Grissom strolled the grounds. The sun was bright, but frost-bound nights had grayed the grass. A breeze delivered a false hint of rain. Mr. Grissom spoke out of the hood of his sweatshirt. "You're getting to be a short-timer, Sawhill. You excited yet?"

"I think of other things," Bobby said. "Who'll take my place in the library? I was thinking maybe Jason."

"Jason reads comic books, not real ones." They were passing the softball field, which had a forlorn look. Weather had expunged the chalk lines. The bases were gone. "You never played ball, did you?"

"I wasn't much good. Dibs was."

"Dibble was a natural. I don't forget what he did, but I can forgive. I care for you boys."

They were walking now in the tattered shadow of the high fence, chain-link, razor wire at the top. Beyond was woodland, and beyond that, unseen, was the other world.

"Who's going to take my place, Mr. Grissom? Who's going to be your eyes and ears?"

"That's nothing for you to worry about."

"Not Jason?"

"I don't think Jason can fill your sneakers, do you?"

"I filled Dib's. Why shouldn't he fill mine?"

Mr. Grissom smiled. "Maybe he will, who knows?"

As they moved away from the shadow of the fence, the sun pinched Bobby's eyes shut. Opening them, blinking, he watched the flight of a crow. "I wish I wasn't leaving," he said.

"Nothing I can do about that. You leave here, it means you're grown up."

"It means I'm a man."

"Yes, it's supposed to."

They headed back to the main building, at a fast clip, their shadows in pursuit. Mr. Grissom had telephone calls to return before day's end, one of them to Bobby's uncle. Before they parted in the reception area, Bobby said, "Do you have Sharon's address?"

"She didn't stay in touch. People don't."

"Will you stay in touch?"

"Best I don't," Mr. Grissom said.

Jason was on his cot. He lay on his side with his palm propping his jaw. He stayed silent for as long as he could and then asked, "What did you and Mr. Grissom talk about?"

Bobby was doing homework, trigonometry, at the writing table. Without looking up, he said, "About when I leave."

"That ain't yet."

"It's not far off."

"They gonna give you a party when you go?"

"They don't do that here."

Jason slowly swung his legs over the side of the cot and sat up. "When you go, what if I can't handle it?"

"You learn to let things roll off you."

"But what if I can't, just can't?"

"I don't know."

A distant bell rang. It meant lights out in Dormitory C. Jason got up and stood behind Bobby. He peered over his shoulder. "Will you miss me?"

Bobby turned a page in his book. "Sure I'll miss

you, but the worst thing will be saying good-bye to Dibs and Duck."

Mr. Grissom had been on the phone with Ben Sawhill for nearly twenty minutes and was beginning to lose his patience. Doodling on a jotting pad, "I don't know what else to tell you. I can't get into the boy's mind."

"I want to know what I'm facing when he gets out," Ben said. "I want to know if I'll be able to sleep at night."

"You see him one way, Mr. Sawhill, I see him another. A gentle boy. He got love here. I'll tell you something else, which I won't go into, he got mothering. That's what I call therapy, the sort similar institutions don't offer. Could I be wrong about him? Of course. What more can I say?"

"You can tell me he won't kill again."

Using the Parker pen Bobby didn't want, Mr. Grissom drew lightning bolts on the pad. "I'm not God, Mr. Sawhill."

CHAPTER THIRTEEN

The Dodge Colt swerved out of the cemetery and bounded at alternating high speeds down Burnham Road, the yellow center line no matter of concern to Mrs. Perrault, nor the stop sign that lay ahead. Chief Morgan pulled her over on Fieldstone Road, just beyond the ice-cream stand. She greeted his approach with a frown of relief.

"I'm glad it's you, not Floyd Wetherfield. He'd likely shoot me." Her voice rose. "Why'd you stop me?"

Morgan was distressed by her appearance, for she had let herself go. Her hair was straggly, the dyes worn away, the white tarnished by age. Her blue eyes were milky. "You were all over the road," he said. "I'm worried about your safety."

"I wish you'd been more concerned with Claudia's. I was at the grave. I told her the boy who killed her is a man now and walking free. Where's he living, James? With his rich uncle?"

Two cars passed. Morgan waved to one of them.

"His father's house, Mrs. Perrault. He's living there alone."

"What are you going to do about it?"

"Nothing I can do." He placed both hands on the window ledge. "I'm not sure you should be driving."

"Are you going to ground me? Am I a child now?"

He listened to the Colt's idling engine. "How's it running, Mrs. Perrault?"

"It'll outlast me. I'll leave it to you in my will, James. Something of Claudia's. Is that a new car you're driving?"

"Relatively. How are your sisters?"

"Being waited on hand and foot at the nursing home. One's crazy, the other's demanding. Ida's the worst. They're waiting for me to join them. No way! I'll follow you home. I'm going to drive by the Sawhill house, see if I can get a look at him."

"Don't do that, Mrs. Perrault. It's only torturing yourself."

"Will you see him?"

"Eventually."

Leaning away from the wheel, she suddenly clamped her hands over Morgan's. "When nobody's looking, use your gun on him."

"I don't carry one," Morgan said.

Ben Sawhill sat in his brother's house, now his nephew's, and tried to look relaxed. A cleaning service had recently gone through each room and left everything fresh and neat. Ben had stocked the refrigerator and cupboard. He gave a start when he heard the toilet flush and forced his face back into a smile when Bobby reappeared.

"You haven't said yet. How's it feel to be home?"

"I don't know." Bobby flopped into an easy chair. He was wearing a short-sleeved shirt and stone-washed jeans, part of a wardrobe Ben had bought for him. "You said you were going to have me over for dinner."

"We are, but Aunt Belle isn't feeling well just now."

"Why haven't the twins come to see me?"

"They're away, Bobby. They're at camp."

Bobby's eyes seemed overly clear. They made Ben think of washed windows reflecting only sky. "Have you given any more thought to what you want to do?"

"No. When can I see my money?"

"I'll go over everything with you. We'll start a checking account you can draw on. While you've been away, your father's holdings have been making money for you. Conservative investments for the most part, a few where the yields have been higher."

"Am I rich?"

"No, but you're comfortable. It doesn't mean, however, you shouldn't give thought to the future. I still think you should consider college."

"I'm a graduate of Sherwood."

Ben kneaded his brow. Without warning he had acquired a migraine, a splitting one, as if a hammer had been laid to his head. "Maybe you'd like to travel?"

"No," Bobby said, a touch of malaise in his voice.

"What do you want to do?"

Bobby's expression was vague.

"I don't know how to help you," Ben said, still pressing his brow. For some reason he remembered the canary he and Belle had given him, a white one with a gray crest, a marvelous singer. He wondered what had happened to it. He remembered showing him a coin trick, one hand conniving with another to pull a quarter from Bobby's ear.

Bobby said, "You hate me, don't you?"

"No. I simply don't understand you. I don't understand why you had to kill somebody. Maybe if I knew that I *could* be of help."

"I don't need any."

Ben dropped his hand and spoke through pain. "You could still be tried for what happened to old Mrs. Bullard. It's not a closed case. That's what Chief Morgan told me. Did you push her down the stairs, Bobby?"

"I don't have to answer questions."

"No, you don't," Ben said, rising with effort. "But you're back in the real world. This isn't Sherwood. The chief isn't Mr. Grissom."

Bobby smiled. "Is he scared of me?"

"We're all scared of you. We don't know what the hell you're going to do."

Bobby said, "I'm going to ride my bike."

* * *

Gloria Eisner spent all of Sunday morning in a continuing attempt to restore what was once a garden. Chief Morgan had stopped by to give her a hand, but he was more hindrance than help, stepping where he shouldn't and pulling up what wasn't necessarily a weed. She was glad he didn't stay long.

At noon she went in to wash up and prepare lunch for her and Trish Becker. Trish, who had invited herself, arrived a little after one. Gloria set the table in the kitchen and served up salad, ravioli, and Italian bread. The ceiling fan moved at half speed.

"I like what you've done with the place," Trish said, "but are you happy here?"

"Do I look unhappy?"

"No, that's what bothers me. I thought you'd miss me."

"I moved out of the Heights, not Bensington."

Trish ate sparingly, Gloria with appetite. Gloria buttered another slice of bread.

"That's what I hate about you," Trish said. "You stuff yourself and never gain an ounce. What's with you and the chief?"

"Dear James is overprotective. He sent someone to check all the locks and made a big deal about the one on the bulkhead."

"That's understandable. Harry's kid is out."

"That's more a problem for James. I'm not foolhardy, but I won't let my life be influenced by some kid I don't know. Besides, most nights James is here."

"So you two have become that thick, huh?"

"It's a life. It's what I want for now. So tell me what's with you?"

"I love my job. I drive into Andover each morning and take Amtrak. Miss all the brutal traffic. I have my own office and share a secretary. No men in my life, and it doesn't bother me."

"So you're happy."

"I'm not overjoyed, but I feel good about myself, better than I have in years. I'm putting my house on the market. I want to live in Boston, a condo on the waterfront."

"Can you afford it?"

"Depends on what I get for the house. Think about it, Gloria. Could be a good move for you. The two of us together again."

Gloria gave her a cynical smile. "We're a couple of ex-school chums, two gals growing old. We'd end up hugging each other in the night."

"That's bad?"

"It's not what I want." Gloria mopped up tomato sauce with her bread and pushed away a clean plate. "Besides, I've started a garden."

Chief Morgan and Ben Sawhill met at a rest area on County Road and stood between their parked cars. Ben's eyes were red from an early exuberance of goldenrod. Morgan's chin was cut from a hurried shave. Neither had a smile for the other.

"The word's got around he's back," Morgan said. "People aren't happy. Meg O'Brien's taken most of the calls. Some are ugly, the rest are scared."

"I blame myself," Ben said. "I should've let him be tried as an adult."

"I blame you too, but that doesn't solve anything. How do you read him?"

"I don't. He speaks mostly with his eyes, and all they do is chill me. I have this crazy feeling he's the player and I'm the toy."

Morgan watched two pickup trucks speed by, one on the tail of the other. "Has he made any threats?"

"None." Ben's face seemed ready to crack from holding the same strained expression too long. "Are we overreacting?"

"What else can we do? I can try to keep an eye on him. Beyond that, I don't know. You have any suggestions, Counselor?"

Ben breathed evenly, to prove to himself he was calm. "None legal. None I'd care to tell a policeman."

Crackling came from Morgan's car. Meg O'Brien was trying to reach him on the radio. "Excuse me."

Ben began moving in the opposite direction, his legs wooden and his shoes weights, as if a dream torn loose from his sleep had trapped him in it, no hope of escape. He emptied his bladder behind a tree.

"Someone heaved a rock through your nephew's window," Morgan said when he returned. "The good news is I have an excuse to post a cruiser in front of his house."

Two afternoons later Bobby Sawhill rode his ten-speed bicycle, the seat heightened considerably, around the green. No one bothered him, but many eyes were on him. Sergeant Avery, who had followed him in his cruiser from Summer Street, was parked near Pearl's Pharmacy. Chief Morgan stood outside the Blue Bonnet. Malcolm Crandall came out of town hall and joined him. Shading his eyes, Malcolm said, "The balls on that little prick!"

"He's not so little anymore," Morgan said. "If you stood up to him, he might get you in a chokehold and not let go. Easier to throw something at his house and hide."

Malcolm stiffened. "You accusing me of throwing that rock?"

Morgan turned on him. "Somebody saw you. You do it again, you and I will be playing poker through the bars after I lock you up. Understood?"

"You protecting him?"

"I'm keeping the peace."

Bobby got off his bicycle, propped it near the entrance to Tuck's General Store, and went inside. Sergeant Avery inched the cruiser to Prescott's Pantry, putting him closer to Tuck's. Morgan ambled up the library and stood near the veterans' memorial, which gave him a clearer view across the green. Holly Pride descended the stone steps of the library and spoke in his ear.

"I've been watching him too. What should I do if he comes into the library?"

"Issue him a card and check out his books," Morgan said. "He's a resident."

Bobby reemerged with a soda can and remounted his bike. A man stepping out of the barber shop stopped in his tracks and stared. Bobby pedaled past Sergeant Avery and headed back toward Summer Street. Morgan cut diagonally across the green to the church and followed the path to Reverend Stottle's house.

Answering his knock, Mrs. Stottle whispered, "He's napping."

"Wake him, please. It's important."

Morgan waited inside the doorway. Reverend Stottle appeared presently, smoothing his sparse hair. One shirtsleeve was rolled to the elbow, the other had unraveled. He smiled with pleasure.

"Emergency, Chief?"

"I want you to visit Bobby Sawhill. I want you to talk to him."

"You bet. Anything special?"

"I want you to find out what's in his head."

Bobby Sawhill was trying to reach his uncle. He finally got him through the Boston number and said, "The window's still broken. Who's going to fix it?"

"I called someone," Ben Sawhill said. "Didn't he come by yesterday?"

"No."

"I'll call someone else. Bobby, have you been phoning my house and hanging up when Aunt Belle answers?"

"No. Who said I was?"

"I was only asking. Is everything going all right?"

"There's always a police car around. When I go out on my bike the policeman follows me."

"Chief Morgan is protecting you. What you have

to understand is that many in town wish you hadn't come back. They think you should've gone somewhere else to live."

"This is my house," Bobby said and consumed the last few drops in the Pepsi can. "Where's my father's car?"

"I sold it long ago. The money's in your investment account. Do you want to learn to drive?"

He hesitated. "Sometime."

"We could get you a car. You might want to do some traveling on your own. See something of the United States."

He heard the ringing of a bell. "I have to go," he said.

Reverend Stottle brought a six-pack of light beer with him, a mistake. Bobby told him he didn't drink beer. The reverend should have brought a quart of ice cream, the kind with three flavors. They were sitting in the kitchen with a box of graham crackers Bobby had taken from the well-stocked cupboard. Munching, Reverend Stottle said, "I used to eat these as a boy. Crackers and milk. My mother had them waiting for me when I came home from school."

Bobby glanced away.

"And I did my homework fast so I could listen to *Jack Armstrong* and *Tom Mix* on the radio."

"I don't listen to the radio. I watch TV. Sometimes I read."

"Television tells you one thing, reading tells you so much more. My favorites were *Huckleberry*

240

Finn and *Tom Sawyer.*" Making himself at home, Reverend Stottle went to the refrigerator, then the cupboard, and poured himself a glass of milk while reaching for another cracker. "Let's get down to business, Bobby. Do you believe in God in heaven and the devil in his den?"

Bobby pushed crumbs into a little pile. "Is there a heaven?"

The reverend deliberated. "I don't want to delude you."

"Will I see my mother again?"

"You carry her in your head and heart as she once carried you in her belly. You two are never apart."

"Sometimes I see her in dreams."

"When you go to sleep at night, Bobby, one world vanishes and another comes into play. Who's to say with absolute certainty which is the real one? I can't. Can you?"

"I like dreams, but not all of 'em."

The reverend dunked a cracker. "What do you believe in?"

"I don't know. Nothing. Oblivion."

"Now you've hit on what we all fear. The zero at the end of life. It turns a cemetery into exactly what it is. Is that the way you feel, Bobby? Are you sometimes aware of an emptiness inside you and the cold draft that comes from it?"

"I don't know."

"Are you never really happy?"

Bobby squeezed up crumbs and ate them off his thumb. "At Sherwood I was."

"Are there angers in your heart you can't explain? I know there are in mine. Mine are at God, and he might not even care. Am I getting closer?"

"I don't know. Maybe."

The reverend winked at him. "I think we speak the same language."

"Do you want some more milk?"

"I better not." The reverend looked at the box of crackers and then at his watch. "I hope I haven't spoiled my dinner. Mrs. Stottle will be mad."

"I eat when I want."

The two of them made their way to the front door, the reverend in the lead. When he opened the door, the warmth of the late afternoon swept in. Officer Wetherfield had replaced Sergeant Avery in the cruiser. A neighbor across the street was peering out her front window.

"Will you come back to see me?" Bobby asked.

"Most certainly," the reverend said.

Using Gloria Eisner's cellular phone, Chief Morgan interrupted Reverend Stottle's dinner. "What's your reading?" he said. "What do you see in him?"

"Darkness."

"I need more than that, Reverend."

"I see death. I see a man-child with one foot still in the womb and the other in the grave. I see myself in him."

"But you don't kill people. I need to know if he's on the edge."

"We're all on the edge, Chief, but most of us are able to keep our balance. The good news is I've made headway with him. We're on the same wave-length. He wants me to visit him again."

"Good." Morgan moved from one window to another and viewed a leafy branch, a patch of sky. Lowering his voice, he said, "See if you can get him to talk about Mrs. Bullard."

When he got off the phone, Gloria said, "What was that all about?"

"Bobby Sawhill."

"Trish's stepson," she said lightly.

"Hard to think of him as that."

"She used to be afraid of him. I don't think she is anymore."

"Then she should be," Morgan said.

Gloria moved close to him, contemplated the lines in his brow and the groove down each cheek. "You're getting to be a habit, James. I don't know if that's good or bad."

"Good for me. I don't know about you."

"We should've met before we were toilet-trained. We might have had a chance."

"We still do," he said. They were talking mouth to mouth, their lips occasionally brushing, a phase of foreplay more intimate than kissing.

"We're from different worlds."

"But you're in mine now," he said.

The telephone rang in the half dark. She grappled with it and finally spoke into it. "For you," she said seconds later and passed it over. Morgan lifted himself out of tortured sheets and sat up. Listening, he frowned.

243

"How did you know I was here?"

"What d'you mean, how do I know?" Randolph Jackson said. "Whole town knows where you're sacking out."

"What do you want, Randolph?"

"I want you to get that goddamn cruiser away from the kid's house. All it does is draw more attention to him and advertise we got a killer in town."

"I'm trying to keep an eye on him."

"Find a better way."

The line dead, Morgan put the phone down, swung his legs over the side of the bed, and sat with his hands on his knees. Gloria's hand crept up his bare back, producing goose bumps.

"Am I making your job harder?"

"Yes," he said. "It's you I'm worried about."

"I'm not Claudia MacLeod."

"I know who you are."

"He doesn't."

Morgan stood up. "He didn't know her either."

"James."

"What?"

"You have a nice ass."

Reverend Stottle brought ice cream, three flavors, which they ate on the back porch, where for a while they simply listened to the eerie stridulation of grasshoppers, which at times seemed to mimic music. The only shade came from a tired maple barely able to put out leaves. Bobby said, "Let's not talk about God."

"He does become tiresome, I admit." Reverend

Stottle, seated on a camp chair, held his dish of ice cream high and was careful not to drip any. "What would you like to talk about?"

"I don't know. Something different."

"How about ourselves? When I was your age, studying for the ministry, I was coping with a desperation I was afraid to give a name. Do you know what it was, Bobby? Sexuality. First I thought I was queer, but I wasn't. I was a mama's boy. Sound familiar?"

"No."

"Then I realized I was preoccupied with women. Their private parts."

Bobby scraped his dish and placed it under his chair. "I know what they look like."

Reverend Stottle ate the chocolate and vanilla portions, saving the strawberry for last. "But am I getting warm?"

"I don't think of those things."

"I keep a private journal so I can dig into myself. Most people are afraid to dig deep, afraid they'll hit mud. Is that what you're afraid of, Bobby?"

"No mud in me."

Reverend Stottle disposed of his dish. "There's mud in all of us. Want me to prove it? Tell me your thoughts when you killed Claudia MacLeod."

"I didn't have any."

The music of the grasshoppers hit high notes, as if someone had turned the heat up. Bobby's face was reddening. The reverend said, "You must have had some when you pushed Mrs. Bullard down the stairs."

"You're trying to get in my mind."

"Aren't you lonely there? Aren't there things you want to tell?"

"I didn't like the flowers."

"What flowers?"

"I don't want to talk anymore."

"I think we should."

Bobby's hand shot sideways and clenched the reverend's wrist. The reverend yelped. The strength of the grip astounded him, the hold on him seemed lethal.

Bobby said, "I don't want you coming back."

Sarah Stottle placed ice on her husband's swollen wrist and told him he was a fool to have gone there. "If I were you," she said, "I'd swear out a complaint. That was an assault."

"I gave him cause. I'm at fault too."

"You're lucky you lived to tell about it."

"I intruded into his private chaos."

"Then you're real lucky."

"I have to call the chief."

"Stay where you are," she said and brought him the phone, then keyed the number for him and hovered.

When the chief came on the line, he said, "You're right to worry."

CHAPTER FOURTEEN

He bicycled through September heat to the Heights and turned up the drive to his uncle's house. Fruit trees he remembered being planted had grown considerably. Apples on the ground were juicing into cider, inebriating hornets. He propped the bicycle near arborvitae. Touch-me-nots cascaded from a hanging pot on each side of the front door. He felt he didn't have to ring the bell. He was family.

He heard no voices.

Paths of sunlight took him through archways into rooms where the furniture was familiar but the arrangement wasn't. In one room he saw on the wall a large framed photograph of his grandfather, whom he knew only by that picture. In another room Dresden porcelain in a china closet caught his attention as it had years ago when he sought meaning in the design on the cups. In the sunroom he saw his aunt.

Aunt Belle was napping, stretched out with one arm folded and the other thrown straight. Her satiny shirt looked like fabric from an undertaker's most expensive casket. Except for stray strands of gray in her black hair, she looked no older from the last time he had seen her. He wanted to lie beside her but knew better.

In a long sitting room he looked out an overlarge window at the swimming pool and saw two female figures on chaises. At first he thought they were naked. They were in bikinis. For more than a moment he could not believe they were Sammantha and Jennifer. They were no longer children.

He entered the pool area through a low gateway. His sneakers marked the wet tiles. At first the twins didn't see him. They were engrossed in themselves, in their chatter. He knew Sammantha by her voice, bigger than Jennifer's. The last time he had seen them was at a Sunday dinner. They were eight or nine, and Sammantha didn't like her dessert and gave it to him. Sammantha noticed him first and sat upright.

"I'm your cousin," he said. "I'm Bobby."

Jennifer reached for a shirt. Sammantha stood up as she was and said, "You look the same but so much bigger."

He smiled. "Aren't you going to kiss me?"

Without hesitation, she pecked his cheek. "Was it bad where you were?"

"No, it was good," he said, his gaze taking in the two of them. Jennifer had drawn back. "You're both so beautiful."

Sammantha grinned. "If one is, the other has to be."

He looked at the pool. "Let's all jump in."

"You don't have a bathing suit."

"I'll go in my underwear."

"No," Jennifer said. "I don't think you should."

"Oh, go ahead," said Sammantha.

They watched him pull off his sneakers, shed his T-shirt, and drop his jeans. Holding his nose, he leaped into the green-blue water and made a tremendous splash, which drove them back. He surfaced with a snort, whipping his hair back. He was not a swimmer, but he kept afloat.

"Aren't you coming in?"

Sammantha would have, but Jennifer clutched her arm. "Mom's coming."

Belle Sawhill strode straight to the pool's edge and told the twins to leave. "Back to the house!" she said when Sammantha was slow to obey. Sammantha gave her a look but joined Jennifer and left. Trembling only a little, Belle said, "Get out of the pool, Bobby." He used the ladder. She was stunned by the size of him, the brawn. "What are you doing here?"

"I came to see my cousins."

"Did you tell your uncle you were coming?"

He shook his head. His genitals, visible through his soaked underpants, were too prominent to ignore.

"Get dressed."

"I'm all wet," he said, and she tossed him Sammantha's towel. He turned his back to her, got out of the underpants, and dried himself with care, almost as if he were performing. "You never invited me to dinner."

"I don't intend to. You're not welcome here."

"The twins got each other. I got nobody."

"That's your fault."

He was in his jeans. Turning, he pulled the zipper up. She kicked his sneakers toward him. She was a lioness protecting her young. "You're a bitch," he said.

"That's right. And I mean business."

His sneakers on, he crouched down and knotted the laces. Rising, he slipped on his T-shirt. "I hate you."

"That doesn't scare me," she lied. "It doesn't even bother me."

A rage built as she escorted him around the side of the house to the front, where she watched him take his time mounting his bicycle. She wanted to attack him.

"Why did you kill those two women? Do you even know?"

He stared at her as if scarcely aware of what she was talking about, the events softened by time, not worth bringing up. She was struck by what she saw in his eyes. He seemed to be expecting a good-bye kiss.

She said, "Don't let me see you here again."

From the Heights he glided down Ruskin Road and steered right onto Spring Street, which bent one way and then another past small neat houses with large front windows. A little white car idled in a driveway and pulled out as he sped by. On Summer Street it bounded after him and would have hit him had he not heard it coming. He swerved sharply and ran the bicycle up onto the sidewalk, where he lost control of it.

The little car, a Dodge Colt, had also gone out of control, jumping the curb and coming to a stalled stop. Bobby walked his bicycle up to it and peered at the driver, an elderly woman with wild white hair.

"Why did you do that? You almost hit me."

The woman didn't speak. Her mouth was aquiver.

"Are you sick?" He leaned closer. "Who are you?"

The woman thrust out a hand and tried to scratch his face. "You don't even know!"

Chief Morgan received calls from two residents of Summer Street, each reporting the incident, each readily naming the bicycler but declining to identify the motorist, mentioning only the size and color of the automobile. Both expressed regret they had no need to call an ambulance. Morgan thanked them for civic responsibility.

Meg O'Brien appeared in the doorway. "Someone to see you."

"I'm not surprised. Come in, Bobby."

Bobby spoke as he entered. "An old lady in a car tried to run me down."

"Good thing she was old," Morgan said. "Younger, she might've got you. Sit down."

Bobby planted himself on a metal chair. "You said anybody gives me trouble I should call you."

"When did I say that?"

"When I was five, almost six."

Morgan sat back in his rotary chair, his elbows on the armrests. "Who was the old lady, Bobby? Do you know?"

"No. But she had funny white hair."

"Who did she remind you of?"

"Nobody."

"You sure? Did she have the rose you gave her when you were twelve, almost thirteen? How do you know it wasn't her?"

Bobby's gaze was steady. "You don't scare me."

"I'm not trying to, but how can I help you if you don't tell me the truth? You want me for a friend or an enemy? That's what it comes down to."

Bobby stood up. "I don't need your help."

Morgan also rose, moved swiftly, and came face-to-face with him. They were the same height. "You hurt anyone again, Bobby, I'll come after you. This time I'll have a gun."

Bobby didn't blink. Nothing in his face moved. It was as if he had accepted a challenge.

Morgan followed him out of his office and watched him leave. Turning to Meg O'Brien, he said, "Call Mrs. Perrault. Tell her she pulls another trick like that I'll take away her license."

In bed Ben Sawhill turned to his wife, but she pushed him away. For a while they lay in silence in the dark. Finally she said, "That's your way of relieving tension, it's not mine."

He had no response, no defense.

252

"Aren't you worried?" she asked.

"Of course I am," he said. "I'm arranging for another lawyer to handle his financial affairs."

"Big deal. That's nothing, Ben."

She turned on her side, her back to him, the covers pulled half over her head, and tried to fall asleep. Ben lay flat, his breathing bothering him from tension in his chest. Both were wide awake when they heard the scream. Belle, out of the bed before Ben could move, knew instinctively which twin it had come from.

Ben behind her, she rushed into Jennifer's room as Sammantha came out of hers. Ben clawed the light switch. Sitting up, her face stark, Jennifer said, "I'm all right."

Belle threw her arms around her. "What happened?"

"I dreamed Bobby killed Sammantha."

Belle, unable to sleep, went down to the kitchen and made coffee. Presently Ben joined her. He looked worse than she did. When he reached across the table for her hand, she withdrew it. "He's poisoned everything," she said. "Even our marriage."

"Don't talk that way."

She scrunched her face up to sip coffee too hot for her lips. "Did you think I didn't know?"

"Know what?"

She left the table, carried her coffee with her, and went to an open window where she laid an ear to the night and heard stray breezes, twitterings, animals coming out of hiding. Ben came up behind her and was going to touch her but pulled back at the last second.

"I want you to do something about him," she said. "I don't care what, I don't care how extreme, but I want you to do something."

"I promise," he said.

Gloria Eisner frowned. The garden was indifferent to her. Rose bushes she'd faithfully watered through the spring and summer showed no gratitude and little growth. Tiger lilies had long ago sulked and died without blooming. Two azaleas were losing their leaves, perhaps purposely. Gloria tossed aside the hose, turned off the water, and said, "Fuck 'em!"

A voice behind her said, "Women shouldn't swear."

She spun around and saw a young man in an open print shirt worn loose over jeans. "Women shouldn't do a lot of things. What are you doing on my property?"

"I came to look at the garden. It's not like I remember."

"I can believe that. If you're done looking, I think you'd better leave."

He started to turn away, then glanced back. "Are you her daughter?"

"Whose daughter?"

"The lady who used to live here."

"No." She regarded him more prudently. "I'm

slow, very slow," she said. "You're Harry Sawhill's son, aren't you? You're Bobby."

He nodded vigorously, as if happy to be recognized. He was wearing something under his shirt, on his belt. She wasn't sure what it was.

She said, "Unless you leave this very minute, I'm going to piss my pants."

He smiled. "You're funny."

"No, I'm telling you the truth. And then I'll scream."

He backed off.

She waited a moment and crept to the gate. He was mounting a bicycle. She watched him ride off and vanish down the street. The woman who lived in the next house appeared on the sidewalk.

"I already called the police."

Gloria latched the gate. "Did you tell them he had a knife?"

Chief Morgan stood on Bobby Sawhill's doorstep, face-to-face with him. They were the same height, though Bobby had the heavier physique. Morgan said, "Lift your shirt."

"I don't have to."

"If you're carrying a concealed weapon I'm arresting you."

Bobby opened his shirt and pulled the tails back. Morgan expected to see a sheathed knife for hunting or fishing, the sort Harry Sawhill might have had in the house. Instead, clasped to Bobby's belt, was a slender flashlight.

255

"What's that for?"

"I hear noises at night. I investigate."

"What kind of noises?"

Bobby shrugged. "I don't know. From the yard."

"Officer Wetherfield tells me he sees you on the green at night, sitting on a bench, midnight or later. What are you doing there?"

"I like to look at the stars. We're all made of stardust, that's what I read. My friend Dibs was coal waiting to become diamond."

Morgan didn't know who or what Dibs was and didn't care to. He said, "You went back to the Bullard house. That's rubbing it in our faces. That's thumbing your nose at the whole town."

"I didn't do anything wrong."

"You trespassed."

"The gate was open. The lady living there told me to leave and I did."

Morgan lowered his voice. "Do you think I'll let you take another woman away from me? No way."

"I don't have to talk to you," Bobby said and, stepping back, closed the door in Morgan's face.

Trish Becker, glad to be home from a busy work-day, shucked off her professional clothes, including her bra, which had left red ridges under her breasts. Views of herself in the triple-paneled mirror in the bedroom pleased her, even excited her, as if her excess weight had turned into an advantage and rendered a truer definition of the woman lurking inside her. She slipped on an outsize sweatshirt and jeans she couldn't button at the top, which didn't matter. She'd buy new ones.

In the kitchen she began making a light supper for herself. Not until she began laying out flatwear did she notice the watch on the table. Harry's Rolex. A voice behind her said, "I don't want it anymore."

She whipped around, yet was calm. "How did you get in?"

"The door was open," Bobby said.

"No, it wasn't."

"Then it was unlocked."

"You're lying on both counts," she said and tried to stare him down, an impossibility.

"I'm not going to hurt you," he said.

"Why would you even say that? I was good to your father. I was good to you." She placed a plate and a water glass on the table. "I'm not afraid of you. Does that surprise you?"

"Good, I don't want you to be." Smiling shyly, he said, "You have big titties."

She gave a start. "You watched me change."

"I won't do it again." He had something vital to ask her, she could see it in his face. He took a breath. "Can I live with you, Aunt Trish?"

She recoiled without showing it. "Why would you want to?"

"I don't feel safe."

"No, Bobby, you can't. The house is for sale. Didn't you see the sign? I'm moving away."

His face went blank with what passed for acceptance. He nodded as if he understood and turned to leave.

"Bobby, why did you kill those women?"

"I don't know," he said. "Nobody ever told me."

From a window she watched him pedal in and out lamplight down the drive and vanish around the stone gateway. Then she went to the telephone, rang up Ben Sawhill, and in a composed voice related everything.

"You're not to worry," he said. "The chief and I have been talking."

"What good's that going to do?"

"We're working something out," he said. "Trust me."

"Belle doesn't. Why should I?"

From a bench on the green Bobby Sawhill engaged in a lonely study of the starlit sky. It was a bright cloud-streaked night in which the moon was a moth snared in a web, a situation Bobby likened to his own. He saw the stars in a more benign light. They were signals, messages, if only he could read them. He wanted Dibs to have been wrong about oblivion. He wanted to believe his mother remembered him.

The swish of footsteps on the grass behind him should have frightened him, but he was too tired and too wrapped in himself. Besides, the voice was his uncle's.

"What are you doing, Bobby?"

"I like to look up."

"Can you name the planets? Can you point out the Big Dipper?"

He shook his head. "I just know what I see."

His uncle, wearing a thick jacket, sat beside him. "I heard about the woman trying to run you down. The chief says you hear noises outside the house. God knows, who's out there. You're right not to feel safe." Ben Sawhill removed something heavy from his jacket pocket. "This is for you, Bobby, in case anyone tries to hurt you. It was your father's."

Bobby looked at it and did not want to take it. It was a snub-nose .32-caliber revolver. "I'll get arrested," he said.

"No, you won't. The chief knows I'm giving it to you. He thinks you should have it too. There's only one round in it. Someone tries to hurt you, you fire it in air. That'll scare whoever it is away." Ben waited. "Don't you want it?"

"I don't know."

"It's up to you, but I think you need it for protection. You're a man now, Bobby. You have to take care of yourself."

His thoughts returned to the sky. One night at Sherwood he, Dibs, and Duck had watched a lunar eclipse, the earth's shadow pilfering the moon. That was how Dibs had explained it.

Ben laid the revolver between them on the bench and rose wearily. "You take it if you want, Bobby. There's only so much I can do for you."

He closed his eyes when he heard his uncle leave. The night air, which hadn't bothered him before, began to creep into his clothes. The moon, escaping the web of clouds, shined bright. Bobby mounted his bike.

Chief Morgan, standing in the dark under the green's single red maple, watched him pedal away. Ben Sawhill surreptitiously joined Morgan, and the two of them headed toward the bench. Neither spoke. Morgan flashed a light on the bench.

Ben said, "He took it."

Chief Morgan and Ben Sawhill had entered into a conspiracy and hoped to draw Reverend Stottle into it. Neither was especially religious, but as if to lessen their load they wanted his blessing, which was the reason they were seated in his study, the door closed. The reverend sensed intrigue and was excited.

"What is it, gentlemen?"

"We have to do something about Bobby," Morgan said, sitting back, one leg athwart the other. His eyes signaled Ben to take over.

Ben spoke from a deep-rooted sigh. "My own nephew, and I'll never know who he is. I don't think he knows either."

"Do any of us?" Reverend Stottle offered. "I look at your nephew and see a lost child who had done evil."

"At Sherwood he could pretend he was still a child. Here, that's impossible. The chief and I are racked with terrible concerns."

Morgan seemed to come out of a trance. "We're sure he'll kill again."

"Oh, dear." The reverend appeared sad but not shaken. "Much of human life is a destructive force."

"We don't know who, when, or where," Morgan said commandingly, "but we have to stop him. Force his hand."

"How do you do that?"

"Provoke him. Ben will explain." Morgan forced himself to his feet. "May I use your bathroom?"

The reverend gave directions, and Morgan slipped away quickly, like a fugitive. The overhead light in the little bathroom infused his face with an unhealthy quality. His gaze into the oval mirror above the sink was cold and rejecting, as if he were confronting another self. Water gushed sideways from the tap. Bending over, he filled his hands and soaked his face.

He took his time returning. Reverend Stottle's expression was strangely serene. Ben, who appeared gutted of all emotion, said, "Austin understands . . . and agrees. It's not a question of right or wrong. It's a matter of the common good, the protection of the innocence."

The reverend nodded. "It's not God's work, it's man's."

"The question," Morgan said, "is whether we have the will to do it. And then if we can live with ourselves."

"I don't think we have a choice," Ben said.

"And you'd like me to be there."

"That's up to you, Austin."

"Yes, I think I should be. It's a mission of mercy."

Morgan spoke sharply. "Let's not kid ourselves, it's murder. But maybe murder for the right reason."

The day had been unseasonably warm, and the night was extremely unsettled, at times tropical. Windows were opened, curtains blowing in. Reverend Stottle and his wife were watching television in the sitting room, though the reverend's mind clearly wasn't on it. He thought he heard birds singing and cocked an ear.

"Weird night," he said.

"No weirder than you," Sarah Stottle said caustically. "You've been at sixes and sevens since dinner. What's the matter with you?"

"The soul is restless." On his feet, he went to the window and bathed his face in dark breezes. "You know, Sarah, I think I may take a stroll around the green."

She viewed him incredulously. "At this hour?"

"I want to look at the heavens, talk to God."

"Cut the shit, Austin. You haven't given him a serious thought in years."

"You're wrong, Sarah. Actually it's the other way around."

At that moment, at his home in the Heights, Ben Sawhill was slipping on a dark athletic jacket. A few hours earlier he had thrown up his dinner, but he was feeling better now and had some of his color back. The twins were in their rooms, and

Belle was reading the current issue of *Vanity Fair*. He looked in on her.

"I'm meeting with the chief," he said.

She looked at her watch. "An odd hour."

"I don't know how long I'll be. Don't wait up."

She turned a page of the magazine. "Anything you want to tell me?"

"I don't think you want to know," he said.

Chief Morgan at that moment was arming himself with a 9mm-semiautomatic pistol he had never fired. The pistol, a replacement for an old service revolver, was a gift from Meg O'Brien several birthdays ago. She thought he should have a proper weapon in the event of emergency. The revolver had never been comfortable on his hip, and neither was the pistol compatible with his underarm. Gloria Eisner, whom he thought was engrossed in a rented movie, came up behind him.

"What have you got there?" Her voice acquired an edge. "I thought you didn't carry a gun."

"Police business."

"Something's wrong," she said, facing him. "What is it?"

He slipped on a windbreaker. "I'm playing God."

"That's a big part. Care to explain?"

"I've never been able to protect my women. About time I did."

Something altered in her eyes, which affected her breathing. "This isn't for me, is it, James? If it is, I don't want it."

"Not *only* for you," he said.

* * *

In the sultry dark Morgan felt like a soldier entering battle, his legs unsteady. In Vietnam he'd looked upon them as temporary, likely to be blown off. Here on the green he cut an uneven path, thwarting imaginary trip mines, and rendezvoused under the red maple, where Ben Sawhill immediately whispered in his ear. "He's here. Same bench."

Reverend Stottle murmured, "He's the wolf, we're the lambs."

Straining his eyes, Morgan made out the shape of Bobby Sawhill's head and the set of his shoulder, nothing else.

"If you're having second thoughts," Ben said, "we can walk away. We can do that right now."

A slash of lightning gave the night a lurid moment of daylight, in which the world looked like bone. The thunder that followed was big and bad. Morgan imagined cats hiding in their fur, dogs cringing, babies bawling. In Vietnam he'd participated in kill counts, women and children included in the totals.

Reverend Stottle said, "What if he fires at us?"

"The gun will make a noise, that's all," Ben said. "The shell's empty."

In Vietnam Morgan had been a grunt. Ben Sawhill, whose service had come later, had been a captain on the adjutant general's staff.

Ben said, "Can you do it, Chief?"

"We'll see."

They moved forward in unison, Reverend Stottle's bearing more military than theirs. He even seemed taller, a Christian soldier. A voice rang out.

"Who's there?"

Ben responded. "It's me, Bobby. Chief Morgan's with me. And Reverend Stottle."

"What do you want?"

Streetlight stretched in far enough so that Morgan could see half of Bobby's face, panic in it, a fear without a name. Reverend Stottle had raised a hand, as if to bless. Ben said, "Chief Morgan's going to take you in. Lock you up."

They all saw Bobby reach into his jacket pocket. They all glimpsed the revolver. Morgan had his pistol out.

"It's now or never," Ben said.

Another flash of lightning, and the world was lurid again. Years shaved from it, eyes youthful, Morgan's angular face was a naked nerve, a Vietnam face, Bensington-born, the military one thing, his sensibilities another. The weapon was a weight.

"Do it, Chief."

Shifting from one altered state to another, he shook his head and proffered the pistol. "I can't. Can you?"

Bobby fired the revolver high into a roll of thunder. In the same instant a uniformed figure sprang up to the left of him, the figure immediately recognizable to Morgan.

"No, Floyd!"

A schooled officer of the law, legs spread and feet set, young Floyd Wetherfield gripped his service revolver with both hands and fired twice. He was saving the chief's life, justifying the chief's faith in him.

Both shots missed.

"Bobby, run," Ben hollered.

CHAPTER FIFTEEN

.

Two days later, the morning brisk and windy, Ben Sawhill and Chief Morgan sat on a bench on the green, the same bench Bobby had occupied. They sat with their shoulders hunched and their coat collars hiked. Each held a paper cup of take-out coffee from the Blue Bonnet. Ben, who sounded bone-weary, said, "I don't know where the hell he is. He hasn't slept in his bed. I don't know if he's been back to the house at all."

Morgan peered into his coffee. "We've had an eye out. No sign of him."

Winds had ripped off the last leaves of the red maple. Small branches soughed, larger ones creaked. Ben said, "What have we done, Chief?"

"I don't know. Probably made it worse."

"We were operating in a moral vacuum. No matter what we did, it wouldn't have been right. Doing nothing wouldn't have been right either."

"You look like hell," Morgan said. "You oughta go home, go to bed."

Ben finished off his coffee and crumpled the cup. When he stood up, the wind yanked at his tie and flipped it over his shoulder. "What could we have been thinking of, Chief?"

"Ourselves."

"You going to be all right?"

"No," Morgan said. "But thanks for asking."

He was sound asleep on the leather sofa in his study when his wife woke him and told him he had a call from Sherwood, from Mr. Grissom. "It's about Bobby," Belle said. "He's there."

"Of course!" Ben said, slapping a hand over his eyes. He went to his desk and took the call. "Thanks for calling, Mr. Grissom. How'd he get there?"

"I have no idea." The voice was professional and aloof. "How do you want to handle this, Mr. Sawhill?"

"I'll come get him."

"I want no trouble."

"I'll bring the local police chief with me, that all right?"

"That's fine. I'll expect you in a couple of hours, no later."

"Mr. Grissom! How is he?"

"I've told him different, but he thinks he can stay."

He cradled the phone and rubbed his brow. Belle, staring at him, said nothing. When he started to speak, she turned her back on him.

* * *

Bobby Sawhill napped in his old room, on what had been Dibble's bunk and later his own. In a dream he was a baby again, talcum on his bottom, mother's kisses on his cheek. Each kiss had the weightlessness of a rose petal. Someone tried to roust him, but he refused to wake up. I'm scared, Mommy, he murmured, and his mother soothed him, neatened his hair. He was in short pants now, though unable to tie his shoes. Mommy did it. Someone pulled at his arms, and his eyes snapped open.

"You don't belong here," Jason said. "And that's my cot now, the other one's Billy's."

Bobby blinked. "Who's Billy?"

"He's new. He's me." Jason stood bare-chested in jeans, his belly a quiltwork of muscle, his skin darker than Bobby remembered. "I'm almost you now," he said proudly. "Mr. Grissom's still thinking it over."

"I won't get in your way," Bobby said softly.

"You can't stay. You're too old."

Bobby eased his legs over the edge of the cot and sat up. The writing table, which had always been neat, was cluttered with comic books and girlie magazines. "I was good to you."

"I'm good to Billy."

Bobby smiled. "Do you still have treats?"

"We haven't had none for a while. Mr. Grissom says there's been budget cuts."

"Who's the Ping-Pong champ?"

"We don't have none." Jason backed off. "I gotta go. Mr. Grissom says you can eat in the dining hall. You can sit at my table."

Bobby nodded. "Thank you."

"It ain't me. It's Mr. Grissom."

Alone, Bobby tidied the top of the writing table, placing the comic books and magazines in near-equal stacks. Fishing in the drawer, he came upon a salted cracker and ate it. He found a notepad that had belonged to Dibble and wrote on it. After that, he shuffled a deck of cards and played solitaire.

They drove south from Bensington and well west of Boston, Ben Sawhill at the wheel, Chief Morgan beside him, Reverend Stottle in the rear. The reverend had spent the morning in the nursing home in Andover, where he had visited Malcolm Crandall's father, a diabetic who had undergone an amputation. Leaning forward, his breath on the chief's neck, he said, "A lonely truth is a one-legged man with nowhere to go and no one to take him there. On a bed pan he thinks he's in the driver's seat, though the only traffic is in himself."

Morgan said, "Cool it, Reverend."

Ben had not wanted him to accompany them, but Morgan had insisted, as if the conspiracy were still in force, their mission of mercy still a fact.

"A truth has no need of clothes. A lie dresses itself to the nines."

His hand firm on the wheel, Ben increased the speed. "What's your point, Austin?"

"While I was visiting old Mr. Crandall the fellow in the next bed expired. I felt privileged to be there. The shocked eyes of the dead see everything and nothing. In that rarified gaze lies the mystery

270

of the universe. Astrophysicists would do well to forget the stars and pluck those eyes out."

"Reverend, shut up," Morgan said.

"No," Ben said, "let him talk. I'm not listening."

"I think we've done your nephew an injustice."

"We've already come to that conclusion, Austin."

"Pound for pound, an invented fear bulks bigger than a real one. A real one has a name. An invented one has a soul. That's why you acted as you did."

Morgan, staring out at the darkening sky, said, "We almost there?"

"Almost," Ben said.

An attendant escorted them to Mr. Grissom's office. Mr. Grissom, clad in a warm-up jacket and sweats, greeted them with professional courtesy and solemnity. He was not happy with the situation. "We've never had a boy come back before," he said.

"Except for the fences," Reverend Stottle said, "it doesn't look like such a bad place."

"I do my best."

Ben said, "Does he know we're here?"

"No." Mr. Grissom came out from around his desk. "He's got it into his head he can stay. I hope he doesn't give us trouble."

"Where is he?"

"In his old room. I'll take you to him." Mr. Grissom led them out of the office and down a corridor. "I can have him subdued if necessary."

"I don't think it will be," Ben said.

Mr. Grissom glanced at Chief Morgan. "Are you armed?"

"No," Morgan said.

"I am," Mr. Grissom said, lifting the bottom of his sweatshirt. They turned a corner and then another. Mr. Grissom opened a door and peered in.

"He's not here, sir," a voice said.

"Where is he?"

Jason rose from his bunk and lowered his voice. "He said he wanted to talk to his pals."

"His pals? What are you talking about?"

"You know, sir." A cryptic look passed between them. Then Jason eased forward with a slip of paper torn from a pad. "Look what he wrote down, sir."

Mr. Grissom held the paper at arm's length. Written in a bold hand was *I forgive me.* He passed it over. "Sounds like he's coming to terms, Mr. Sawhill. Why don't you keep it?"

They trooped down another corridor, Mr. Grissom in the lead, a bounce to his step, the others a length behind. Reverend Stottle huffed to keep up. Jason and an attendant had joined in. Mr. Grissom glanced over his shoulder.

"He's in the toilets, what we call the toilets. It's a communal washroom. If you hear him talking and no one's there, don't be concerned. It's a game."

Ben lengthened his stride. "I thought he was talking to his pals."

"They're not here anymore. They're gone."

Mr. Grissom threw open the door to the toilets, barged in, and stopped in his tracks.

Ben Sawhill gasped.

Reverend Stottle stared up at the eyes.

"Someone get a knife and cut him down," Chief Morgan said.

EPILOGUE

Living and working in Boston, her daytime mind constantly challenged, Trish Becker felt intellectually fulfilled. Her large pale body, however, seemed in hibernation, wintering toward an uncertain spring. In the spring she became involved with a widower she'd met through a dating service. He was quiet, unoffending, and reasonably well-off, but each had reservations. She did not consider him up to the mark. He doubted she would wear comfortably. They married anyway. The overriding factor was that each wasn't getting any younger. Each knew panic in the night.

Gloria Eisner did not remarry. Her body had pleased three husbands, none deserving. Her feelings for Chief Morgan, warm but ambiguous, did not prevent her from leaving Bensington permanently when her father died. She moved to New Jersey to be with her mother, a situation that gradually grew unsatisfactory. Each got on the other's nerves. Before another winter set in, she drove to Key West, where her friend Barry greeted her exuberantly. "I came back for the sunset," she said. "Is it still here?"

During a Sunday sermon Reverend Austin Stottle caused considerable stir when he posed two questions. How many generations does God go back? And are there monkeys in his past? A great number of men and women in the congregation demanded he step down, but a few loyal supporters, Ben Sawhill among them, pointed out that he was merely passing through one of his phases. The next Sunday, after a long discussion with his wife, he told the congregation that each day of the year, sunny, stormy, whatever, was a poem written by God.

Ben Sawhill took a leave of absence from his law firm and, avoiding mirrors in the morning because his face didn't look plausible, grew a beard. The twins liked it. Belle did not. The twins worried him. They were obsessed with the thought that if one died, the other would die twice. He was also concerned about his relationship with Belle. They seemed to have grown apart. "Do you blame me for anything?" she asked, and he assured her he didn't. She seemed unconvinced. His most peaceful times were during solitary walks in the woods, where he visualized a world in which time could be rewound and lives relived with a sure sense of what to avoid, happiness a given.

* * *

Bobby Sawhill was buried next to his mother in Burnham Road Cemetery. Mrs. Perrault, a faithful visitor to her daughter's grave, occasionally visited his. Exhausted, she seemed to have forgiven him, though she still murmured, "Why?"

Mrs. Bullard's old house, standing vacant, once again the property of the bank, caught fire one night and burned nearly to the ground. A few in town believed that Chief Morgan was responsible. They claimed that Officer Floyd Wetherfield, who owed his job to the chief, lit the match.

James Morgan, despite occasional controversy, remained police chief of Bensington.

DAVID LAWRENCE

CIRCLE
OF THE
DEAD

The man died of a broken heart. Literally. But what broke his heart was a sharp object shoved hard between his ribs. When they found him he was sitting in a circle with three other corpses in a London apartment. That's when Detective Stella Mooney got the case. Suffering from brutal nightmares and a fondness for too much vodka, Stella's trying to hold it together long enough to find the answers to this bizarre puzzle. But the closer she comes to cracking the case, the more her personal life seems to fall apart. From the glamorous homes of the wealthy to the decidedly tougher parts of town, Stella has to follow the evidence—even when it seems to be leading her in circles.

ALAN RUSSELL
MULTIPLE WOUNDS

Holly Troy is a beautiful and talented sculptor whose only sanctuary is her art. She also lives with dissociative identity disorder, her personality split into many different and completely separate selves—including a frightened five-year-old girl. But now Holly's gallery owner has been found murdered, surrounded by Holly's sculptures. Holly doesn't know if she was a witness to the crime, or if she committed it. She doesn't know where she was that night. She doesn't even know *who* she was.

PREDATORS & PRAYERS

PHILIP CARLO

Someone is brutally murdering priests in New York City. The killer seems to be everywhere at once, striking almost at will. With pressure mounting, the mayor, the governor and the police commissioner all want this madman stopped before one more body is found. But they're not the only ones. The Church and the Vatican need to have the killer silenced, for he is their worst nightmare come true—the living embodiment of a terrible, dark secret.